W9-CLD-860

MacKinnon

Center Point
Large Print

Also by Johnny D. Boggs and available from
Center Point Large Print:

And There I'll Be a Soldier
Top Soldier
Return to Red River
Hard Way Out of Hell
The Kansas City Cowboys
Wreaths of Glory
The Raven's Honor
Poison Spring
Taos Lightning
Greasy Grass

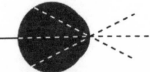

This Large Print Book carries the
Seal of Approval of N.A.V.H.

MacKinnon

Johnny D. Boggs

CENTER POINT LARGE PRINT
THORNDIKE, MAINE

This Circle Ⓥ Western is published by
Center Point Large Print in the year 2018 in
co-operation with Golden West Literary Agency.

First Edition
December, 2018

Printed in the United States of America
on permanent paper.
Set in 16-point Times New Roman type.

ISBN: 978-1-64358-031-9

Library of Congress Cataloging-in-Publication Data

Names: Boggs, Johnny D., author.
Title: MacKinnon : a Circle V Western / Johnny D. Boggs.
Description: First Edition. | Thorndike, Maine :
    Center Point Large Print, 2018.
Identifiers: LCCN 2018040976 | ISBN 9781643580319
    (hardcover : alk. paper)
Subjects: LCSH: Large type books. | GSAFD: Western stories.
Classification: LCC PS3552.O4375 M33 2018 | DDC 813/.54—dc23
LC record available at https://lccn.loc.gov/2018040976

For Eugene Manlove Rhodes, "Pop" Sherman,
Alfred E. Green, Frances Dee, and Joel McCrea

Pasó Por Aquí

CHAPTER ONE

If luck favored him, Sam MacKinnon wouldn't be lynched. The posse from Bonito City might just shoot him.

He lay between a large boulder and a fallen, rotting pine, about thirty feet below a handful of angry riders. They might not see him, but to MacKinnon that seemed a forlorn hope.

"Well?" a man bellowed high above MacKinnon's hiding place.

Just one word, but MacKinnon recognized that Southern drawl, which almost caused MacKinnon to suck in a deep breath. Luckily, he stopped himself because expanding those lungs would likely have left him crying out, writhing and cursing.

"I'm waiting." Nelson Bookbinder sounded touchy today. MacKinnon couldn't blame him, though, as MacKinnon and four others had stopped the Lincoln County sheriff from having his breakfast this morning. Bookbinder, who also served as a deputy United States marshal, said: "What is it?"

"Some blood."

From the guttural answer MacKinnon knew that Bookbinder's Mescalero Apache Indian was scouting for the sheriff. MacKinnon thought he had seen Bookbinder and the Mescalero in Bonito City that morning, but prayed he had been wrong. Now he knew just how much his luck had soured.

"How much blood, Nikita?" Bookbinder asked.

I'm dead, certain sure. MacKinnon's shoulders sagged. Nikita. The Mescalero with the Russian name. MacKinnon was doomed. The best lawman in New Mexico Territory, *and* the best tracker in the Southwest.

The Apache had no chance to answer. "Blood?" another posse member sang out. "Mort, that means we nicked one of 'em back in Bonito City. I told you I hit one of 'em rapscallions."

"Did not. I seen one of 'em bandits almost fall out of his saddle when *I* fired."

"Like . . ."

"Shut up, Davis. You, too, Mort!" Bookbinder yelled. "Not one more word. You boys are so loud you'd startle a deaf man." Bookbinder had to catch his breath. That figured. Pushing sixty years old, Bookbinder had ridden hard out of Bonito City, and climbing high into these rugged mountains left everyone short of breath. After a hard chase out of the mining camp and all the way here, the horses of the posse also labored for breath.

The Apache now answered the sheriff's question. "Not much blood."

"What do you think?" the lawman asked.

A long silence followed. Finally, the Mescalero said: "*¿Quién sabe?* They pay you to think." The voice was rasping, but not the chopped-up English the authors had Nikita speaking in those Beadle & Adams penny dreadfuls. The man was educated.

"Don't get smart, Nikita."

Hell, Nikita's smarter than me. MacKinnon grinned at the thought. What was that Carefree Dan Carter called it? Gallows humor. Which would be just about right, if Bookbinder's posse bothered building a gallows.

"Well," the Apache said, "there's not much blood. Could've come from a horse or a man, but I don't think it's from a bullet or buckshot."

Someone—most likely the man named Davis who had falsely taken credit for winging MacKinnon—cursed.

"Four riders went east," the Apache said at length. "Another horse rode down . . . there."

"Split up?" Bookbinder asked.

"No," the Apache replied. "A *horse*. Without a rider."

This Mescalero is good, MacKinnon thought to himself. *Real good. But everyone in New Mexico Territory, or anyone who had picked up one of those half-dime novels, knows that.*

Bookbinder offered a theory. "So one horse now carries two riders?"

MacKinnon had to breathe in deeply. Tears

9

welled in his eyes as the ribs on his right side sent pain rippling up and down his side.

"No," the scout answered the lawman.

"So what are you telling me?" Bookbinder demanded.

"I'm not telling you a damned thing," the Apache said. "Except this . . . a little blood on rock and pine needles up here. One horse goes this way, without a rider. Four horses go that way, carrying no extra weight. They stopped here. Cinched up. Rested. Reloaded. Horses pranced around, dropped some apples, emptied their bladders. And a lot of rocks and dirt went falling down . . . there."

This is it. MacKinnon's fists clenched.

"All right, Nikita," Bookbinder said. "Spill it. But be quick."

MacKinnon started thinking about how he should play his hand when the posse found him.

"Man dismounts to tighten his cinch," Nikita said. "Gets hit. Falls down the ridge. Horse bolts . . . that way. Other four ride off."

"Why?"

"Sign rarely tells why."

"They split up," the one named Mort offered. "Maybe that *hombre* took the money."

"How can you tell all that?" Davis asked. "I don't see nothing but pine cones, dirt, rocks, and horse apples."

"Shut up," Bookbinder said.

The lawman had to be thinking now, and probably staring down the ridge, maybe looking right at the boulder MacKinnon hid behind. He did not move. He tried to breathe as lightly as he could, ignoring the ants crawling over his face, drawn by the blood seeping from his head.

"So one of the robbers hit this fellow while he's adjusting his saddle, sent him rolling down the ridge. A double-cross. Something like that, Nikita?"

"Maybe so."

"Could that man have caught up his horse? Doubled back?"

"*¿Quién sabe*? I'd have to go down and look."

Nelson Bookbinder swore a little harder this time.

Mort's voice, not Nelson Bookbinder's, bounced off the pine trees and the mountains. "Those robbers taken us for thousands of dollars and . . ."

"You don't know what the Sam Hill you're talking about, Mort," Bookbinder said. "A thousand dollars my arse."

"But that fellow could have rid off with the money they stole," Davis suggested. "Figure we'd ride after the others. And without money, we couldn't prove they done nothin'."

"That's right," Mort said. "They wore wheat sacks over their heads. Nobody saw no brands on the horses or nothin'. Happened too fast."

11

Now, the old law dog filled his ancient lungs with oxygen, exhaled, and the saddle creaked underneath him. MacKinnon heard all of that from his hiding place. Soon, they would find him. Unless they were blind. And nobody ever called Nikita or Bookbinder blind.

"You boys need to shut up," Bookbinder said. "If one of those boys is down there, he can hear everything you're saying."

"Well . . . ," Mort stopped.

Davis didn't. "Then he can hear you, too, Sheriff. And he can even hear that Apache."

"I want him to hear me, you fool!" Bookbinder thundered. "Hey down there!"

His voice echoed. MacKinnon tasted sweat and blood.

"This is Nelson Bookbinder." The name bounced off the mountains. "Sheriff of Lincoln County. If you're smart, you'll give yourself up. It'll go easier on you. You don't want to make me mad-*der.* I'm already mad."

The echoes faded, and the lawman spit and called out: "Think straight, you idiot! Give up!"

A man doesn't think straight when he's broke and hungry.

That's what MacKinnon tried to tell himself, and had been trying to tell himself since this morning. He wondered how Nelson Bookbinder would react to such an excuse. Not that the men

12

from Bonito City would give him any chance to talk. No, they'd just shoot him dead, but that, MacKinnon thought, would be more merciful than stringing him up in one of these tall pines that had not been struck by lightning, that had not fallen near a big boulder, and had not become rotted and infested with bugs.

MacKinnon kept his head down. He did not look up toward the ridge, toward Nelson Bookbinder and that Apache scout. Not that MacKinnon could see above the boulder anyway. Looking up could get a man killed. If he looked up, he would have to lift his head, and that Mescalero probably could see through granite. He certainly could hear anything out of the ordinary.

Four men. MacKinnon expected a lot more riders, but from the penny dreadfuls MacKinnon had read, Bookbinder never liked big posses.

Above, a horse started to urinate, and Bookbinder swore.

"Mort," the lawman said. "You and Davis head down there. See if you can pick up the trail. Maybe one of those curs is dead down there. If he's dead, bring the corpse to Bonito City. I'm sure Charley The Trey will pay you a reward. If he's alive, take him to Lincoln. And keep him alive."

"Aw, Sheriff, you . . ."

"Your ears need cleaning?"

"No, sir," Mort said humbly.

"If we can't find nothin'?" Davis asked.

"Catch up with Nikita and me or ride back to Bonito City. Which way?"

"East," the tracker said.

"Mexico's south."

The Apache laughed. "Before Mexico there's the reservation. White men don't ride through there."

"You boys want to argue some more?" Bookbinder demanded. "Because four of those gents are riding hard away from us, maybe getting away, and if I can't shoot them, I'll settle for rubbing you two out."

Saddle leather creaked again, followed by the metallic clicking of a repeating rifle being levered. "If we hear gunshots, we'll ride back to help you boys," Bookbinder said, softer this time. "Good luck."

MacKinnon kept his face buried in the pine straw and dirt, which cooled his face, his neck, and his chest. Much cooler than the rest of MacKinnon's body felt. At least, that's what MacKinnon kept trying to tell himself.

The scout grunted and swung onto his horse. Mort and Davis mumbled something MacKinnon couldn't catch. Metal hoofs clanged against rocks and crushed pine cones.

Two horses rode off. MacKinnon could not relax. A rock tumbled down the ridge, and Mort and Davis began coming down the slope toward

14

MacKinnon, alone, head bleeding, unarmed, without a horse, without a chance.

Each second felt like a million years.

MacKinnon kept his face so close to the earth, he breathed in dirt and dust. A thousand legs of myriad insects prickled his skin, but he refused to lift his head off the stinking ground. He tried to keep his nerves under control, tried to keep his breaths regular, and tried, desperately, not to scream.

MacKinnon made himself wait.

The breath from his nostrils carved little ditches in the ground. He thought he could count all the grains of sand that he blew into little mounds beside pine cones, pine straw, and tiny pebbles. Trying to focus on those, MacKinnon blocked out the images of those two posse members from Bonito City. He watched the miniscule trench become deeper and the tiny mound climb higher as he breathed—and each breath in and out hurt his busted ribs.

He blinked. Ants and other insects scurried about. Beads of sweat rolled off his forehead, toward his eyes.

He waited. He listened.

"What do you think?" Davis asked. The closeness of the voice startled MacKinnon. They had to be right around the boulder.

"I ain't no Apache," Mort said, cursing and kicking a stone. "Horse took off yonder way."

"Carrying a man?"

"The Apache said no. I ain't no tracker."

Footsteps moved away from the boulder toward the north. Which wasn't necessarily a good thing. If one or both men got far enough away and over to one side, they'd be able to spot him, and Sam MacKinnon would be a dead man. MacKinnon considered praying.

One of the men cursed, sighed, and stopped walking.

"If that man's still here, he could be behind any rock, any tree," Mort said.

Davis agreed. "Might have us in his sights right now."

"The money's with 'em other four boys," Mort said.

"How do you know?"

"Because, by God, Nelson Bookbinder rode after them, not this fellow." Mort spit and added: "And Charley The Trey said he'll pay for the return of the money and the robbers."

They must have reached an understanding silently because the boots moved faster now, heading back. MacKinnon tensed. Maybe they had spotted him and were trying to give him the impression they were leaving. He closed his eyes, remembering when he and his sister played hide and seek. He thought if he closed his eyes, his sister couldn't see him.

Gravel and stones began spilling down from

above. Mort and Davis had to be climbing back up, toward their horses. They were talking, but MacKinnon only heard bits and pieces, followed by the sound of someone stepping into a saddle. A horse snorted.

"Let's wait a while," Mort said.

So MacKinnon lay there, hurting, bleeding, grimacing when some bug would bite him, but he never cried out. Never slept. Certainly could not relax. Five minutes. Then . . . MacKinnon wasn't sure. Fifteen? Thirty?

Suddenly, a rifle shot ripped through the hills and forests, echoing off the rocks. MacKinnon jerked, tightening his eyes shut as spasms of pain shot through his right side.

A warning shot?

Have they seen me?

Nelson Bookbinder and the Apache would be returning at a gallop. Maybe, MacKinnon thought, if he could just run farther into the woods, down the mountain, find a cave or some sinkhole to hide in. Maybe. . . . But that, he understood, would require him to stand up. To move.

He turned his head toward the sound of the gunshot. The horses started moving, but not toward the rotting tree and the boulder.

Lying on his left side, then back on his stomach, MacKinnon waited and listened. The hoofs moved into a fast walk and faded away.

Silence returned to the mountain forest. MacKinnon tried to comprehend what that rifle shot could have meant. He still thought the lawman would return to kill him or haul him to jail. Only when a mountain jay began singing did MacKinnon begin to think he might be safe.

Gingerly, he rolled over, brushed the ants off his face, cringing at the pain in his side. Bracing his back against the cold stone of the boulder, he clutched his right side with his left hand, and gently touched the cut above his right eye. Somehow, he managed to untie his bandanna and pressed one end of it against his head to stanch the blood.

His throat felt like sand.

Sweat trickled into the cut, burning like fire, down his scraped cheeks.

He stared at the pines and the rocks. A painter, a photographer, a minister, or just about anyone would have found this place beautiful. Towering firs and pines rustled in the wind, and rolling hills climbed in the cloudless blue sky. MacKinnon might have found it pretty, too, except for the trouble he found himself in.

Two or three ribs had to be cracked, if not broken. He had no gun, only a folding knife in his trousers pocket, and just fishing that old thing out would hurt like the devil. No canteen, no water, and he'd have a long, hard climb back to the Río Bonito. Maybe those boys in the posse were right. Maybe no one would recognize MacKinnon as one of the robbers. But a stranger, horseless, with an empty holster on a shell belt, with a cut across his head and busted-up side. That would arouse a lot of suspicion, and Charley The Trey probably would need no more evidence to order a hemp party.

It was, MacKinnon decided, a rather pretty place to die.

Still, he halfway wished that the posse had found him and put him out of his misery.

For now, this second, MacKinnon was safe.

Safe? That was a good joke. Safe? Far from it.

He wet his cracked lips, and he spoke in a hoarse whisper. "Lord, there ain't nobody having a worse run of luck right this minute than James Samuel MacKinnon."

CHAPTER TWO

"What you digging?"

Katie Callahan closed her eyes and drove the pickaxe into the sunbaked ground. The metal rang out and the wooden handle vibrated with such force, she had to let go and shake feeling back into her fingers.

"A well?"

Once her eyes opened, Katie sighed, and looked at her little brother. "No." Her voice sounded so hoarse, so desperate. She stood in the middle of the desert, her lungs heaving, her hair and dress drenched in sweat.

"What then?" Gary asked.

A grave. Katie ran her tongue over cracked lips. "Nothing," she said.

The five-year-old jumped into the hole that Katie had started hours ago. When she saw how little she had managed to dig, Katie practically laughed. Hole? Grave? It wasn't deep enough to cover an anthill.

"I wish it was a well," Gary said. "I'm thirsty."

After wiping sweat off her face with her sleeve, Katie lifted her hands, palms up. Splinters freckled her hands where the blisters did not. Blood stained her fingertips. She coughed, glanced at the pickaxe and the shovel, and found her baby brother again.

"Do like I tell you," she said. "Put those pebbles under your tongue. Swallow what spit you can."

"Spit tastes nasty."

Her chest still heaved. She tried to smile, but she failed. "You're a boy. You're supposed to like nasty things."

"I ain't supposed to eat dirt."

"Just do as I tell you. And get back by the wagon, in the shade, out of the sun."

She made herself grab the handle of the pick-axe, cringing at the pain, but she did not have enough energy to lift it right now. She rested, breathing in and out, aching all over.

"Can't I have some water?" Gary whined.

"Later. We have to save it."

"Till Pa comes back?"

The pickaxe dropped to the sand. "Your pa," she snapped before she could stop herself. "Not mine. Not Florrie's."

"Better not say that." Gary wagged his little finger up at Katie's face. "Pa don't like it when you say that. He'll beat you when he comes back."

She laughed slightly. *Like he's coming back.*

"I'm gonna tell Pa what you said. And I'm gonna laugh when he whups you."

If her muscles would co-operate, she might have clenched her fists, but then she probably could not unclench them. And this grave would never get finished.

Gary kept acting like the annoying brother he was. Stepbrother, she told herself, and hated herself for even thinking that. You didn't have any say in picking your parents. Parents didn't pick their kids, unless they were orphans who happened to get adopted.

She thought: *Are we orphans now?* Her head shook. *I'm too old to be an orphan, but* . . . She considered her sister and her stepbrother . . . no, her brother. Shaking her head, she tried to clear away those thoughts. Such things did not matter. Not now.

"Gary . . ." She tried a different approach. "It's hot. I'm tired. And I've got work to do. You'll get water later. Please. Go help Florrie. Go help . . ."

"Ma's still asleep," Gary said. "Florrie's still crying."

"I can hear her." Katie filled her lungs with hot, dry air, and wondered if her nose would start bleeding again. She pulled the bonnet from her head and wrapped it over her right hand, the one with worse blisters and more splinters. The sweat stung, but she bit her lip and just kept wrapping the cotton tighter and tighter.

"Is Ma still sick?" Gary asked.

"Not anymore," Katie said. She tied off the bonnet, and gripped the pickaxe. "Get under the wagon or in the back with Florrie. Go. Now. Do like I tell you."

"Can I hold Ma's hand?"

"Yes." Her shoulders sagged. "She'd like that, Gary. She'd like that a lot."

"Maybe Ma would like some water."

"Get!" she barked, and the boy jumped back. "Now. I've got work to do. Go. Go with Florrie and Ma. You'll get water with the rest of us this evening."

"I'm gonna tell Pa!" the boy whined, but at least he was running back to the wagon.

"He's not my pa!" Katie barked, and managed to lift the pickaxe over her shoulder and bring it down hard into the desert ground. "And he's never been a pa to you, either," she added, but not loud enough for Gary to hear.

She hated herself for saying that. Of course, she had hated herself for some time now, but she despised someone else even more.

The pale rock took a new form. It shaped itself into the weasel face of Thomas "Tommy" Truluck, with the dark eyes too close together, the cheeks and chin covered with pockmarks, the crooked nose, the big ears, the hair that never looked clean, and the peach fuzz that barely amounted to a mustache but what he considered a tonsorial artist's masterpiece.

The pickaxe slammed into Tommy Truluck's right ear, the one that hung lower than the left.

23

The axe came up and struck into her stepfather's bloodshot eye. The iron bit into the broken incisor of the worthless excuse of a husband and father. It cut his greasy hair. Again. Again. Again. Again. She cursed and swung, swung and cursed, until she found herself on her knees, her skirt ripped, and her hands as raw as her throat. The wind blew, hot and hard, and she sank into the dirt. She spit out the pebbles she had put underneath her tongue. Her lungs burned. She heard the angels singing.

Rock of Ages, cleft for me,
Let me hide myself in Thee;
Let the water and the blood,
From Thy riven side which flowed,
Be of sin the double cure,
Save me from its guilt and power.

Rolling onto her back, feeling that furnace of a sun broil her already sun-burned face, she made herself look into the eyes of St. Peter, or Jesus, or the devil himself. Whoever it was to judge her, but no archangel or demon or Redeemer stared at her. She saw a sky that looked white, and the voice she heard came from no angel.

God gave Florrie the voice. And the beauty. Her twelve-year-old sister sang. Ma always said that Florrie sounded like an angel. And it was Sunday.

Not the labor of my hands
Can fulfill Thy law's demands;
Could my zeal no respite know,
Could my tears forever flow,
All could never sin erase,
Thou must save, and save by grace.

More than once Ma had also said: "Florrie, promise me you'll sing at my funeral."

"God!" Katie brought her right arm over her eyes. She had told herself she would not cry, that she could not cry. She just wanted to dig this miserable grave. Mostly, she wanted to kill Tommy Truluck for getting them out here, in the middle of desert. For making them leave Medicine Lodge.

The dry climate, Margie. That's what you need. Clear up them lungs. Sell the store. We'll use the money to get me, you, and the kids down south to New Mexico Territory. There's gold down there. We'll make our pile. Get you back on your feet. It's like paradise, Margie.

"Shut up," she told the voice, the awful memory. "Shut up."

The voice did not listen. It never listened.

Ma had listened to Tommy Truluck, however, and they had left Kansas. They had taken the old Santa Fe Trail and the Cimarron Cutoff all the way to Santa Fe. From that dirty little town of adobe, mountains, and food spiced with chile peppers, Tommy Truluck had led them from one mining camp to another. Elizabethtown . . . Cimarron . . . San Augustine, where Gary was born . . . Georgetown . . . Silver City . . . Hillsboro . . . Chloride . . . Vera Cruz . . . Fairview . . . White Oaks. Always getting there too late to find much pay dirt. At least, that's how Tommy Truluck explained things. It had to do with bad luck, poor timing, cheating thieves, but never Tommy Truluck's laziness, his taste for ardent spirits and loose women, and his inability to recognize that he had no skill at faro or roulette. Town to town, camp to camp, living in tents or in a wagon like the one Tommy Truluck had left them. Till finally he had decided that there was no fortune to be found in New Mexico Territory but he had heard good things about this place down in Texas. A town called Shafter. He had talked Katie's mother into heading across this furnace to Roswell. From there they'd just follow the road south and find a paradise and their fortune in the Chinati Mountains.

They had made it here. Nowhere. Perdition. Hell. A vast expanse of sand and rocks where even the cactus looked dried up and about to die. Till Tommy took a mule, a Henry rifle, saddlebags filled with most of the food he could carry, and three canteens, two filled with water, one with whiskey, or whatever whiskey he had not consumed over those long miles from White

Oaks. He left them with a wagon with a busted wheel, one old mule—the blind one named Bartholomew—the tepid, iron-hard water left in the two barrels, a shotgun (likely because he couldn't carry everything), and the promise that he would send help as soon as he reached Roswell.

Nothing in my hands I bring,
Simply to Thy cross I cling;
Naked, come to Thee for dress,
Helpless, look to Thee for grace:
Foul, I to the fountain fly,
Wash me, Savior, or I die.

Katie made herself stand. She glanced at the sun, and figured it would be behind the mountains in another hour. The air would cool then. Maybe, she told herself, the ground would become softer at dark. She let out a hopeless chuckle, and moved toward the back of the covered wagon.

She looked inside and saw her kid sister and brother. She saw her mother, so pale, so cold, so suddenly ancient-looking, and Katie let herself join in on the last verse, even though she could hit no note or carry any tune.

While I draw this fleeting breath,
When mine eyes shall close in death,
When I soar to worlds unknown,

See Thee on Thy judgment throne,
Rock of Ages, cleft for me,
Let me hide myself in Thee.

Florrie and Gary turned to stare out of the wagon at Katie.

"I've heard dogs howl that sound better than you do, Katie," Gary said, and giggled.

Katie glared, but held her tongue, and she shot her sister a look that silenced Florrie before she could rebuke, or slap, Gary. It wasn't the insult that bothered Katie, or Florrie, for that matter. Tommy Truluck always used that "dogs-howling" insult whenever Katie tried to sing, or whenever their mother could somehow manage to drag Tommy and the kids to a revival meeting or church services in some raw-boned mining camp.

"I'm . . ." She turned away from her mother's lifeless body. "You two need some water."

"You said . . ."

"I know what I said, Gary. One ladle. That's it. Just one ladle. Then you can have some more before we go to bed. You, too, Florrie. Go on."

"Can I bring Ma some?" Gary asked.

Florrie squeezed her eyes tight. "I'll take care of Ma, Gary. Go on. Help your sister. That's it." She tried to smile, but could not remember how.

The boy let go of Florrie's right hand when he came to the opening in the canvas. Katie lifted her weary hands up to help the boy down, but he stopped when he saw the makeshift bandage covering her right hand and the raw flesh on her left.

"Let me jump," Gary said.

"Be careful," Katie said as she stepped back. The boy leaped, landed, and rolled over more times than he should have, but came to his feet, laughing. "That was fun."

Katie nodded. "You all right?"

"I'm thirsty."

"One ladle. Don't spill any." She moved back to the wagon and offered to help Florrie.

"I can manage," her sister said.

"You don't want to jump?" Katie tried.

Florrie stared hard.

"I was just trying to . . ."

"I know what you're doing, Katie. But you'll have to tell him the truth soon."

Katie moved to the side of the wagon. "Wait a minute, Gary. Let Florrie get the water." What had she been thinking? Letting a five-year-old get precious water. He'd let the ground soak up a full cup. "Stop. Stop! Florrie will get you the water!"

She turned, and leaned against the tailgate. Florrie had managed to climb to the ground.

"You need water, too," Florrie told her.

"Later," Katie whispered.

CHAPTER THREE

All those mornings, MacKinnon thought, *after a night of John Barleycorn, when climbing out of my bunk with my head splitting and vomit crusted on my face was the hardest thing I'd ever managed. . . .*

He gasped as, gripping a convenient handhold in the boulder over his head, he pulled himself to his feet. He stood. Well, he leaned against the boulder, at least, and waited for the world to stop spinning and for the gall to sink back down his throat and into his gut, which would start rumbling again any minute.

A pretty place to die, maybe, but MacKinnon had no intention of dying just yet. For one thing, Sheriff Nelson Bookbinder had led that first posse out of Bonito City, but Bookbinder's might not be the only one. Charley The Trey had put up a reward, so that would send every out-of-work miner and ne'er-do-well from Lincoln to White Oaks chasing after those cut-throats who dared to rob the Three of Spades Saloon. From what MacKinnon had heard about Charley The Trey, the cheating gambler might be riding hard right about now. And MacKinnon and his *compadres* had not had any time to cover their trail when they left Bonito City at a high lope.

30

Compadres?

MacKinnon spit at the thought. That hurt, too, and most of the saliva dribbled down his vest and shirt. He rubbed the rest of it off his lips, and checked to make sure he didn't find any blood in the spit.

Swallowing hurt. Breathing hurt. The hard granite bit into his back and his hips. Standing upright hurt. He couldn't bear the thought of actually taking a step or two. But he had to.

Something made him move away from the boulder. He paused, waiting to fall over unconscious or dead, yet he remained upright. His left foot slid from the rotting tree, followed by his right, and something still kept him from keeling over. Something. No, that wasn't right.

Someone.

"Jace," MacKinnon said. He saw Martin's face. "I'm coming."

He managed another step. And another. The face laughed at him. The face mocked him. MacKinnon eased air in and out of his lungs, and took yet another step.

He remembered.

"A saloon?" Chuckling, MacKinnon shook his head, and raised the tin cup of Old Overholt in toast or salute. "Well, that's different." The rye scalded his lips and torched his throat on the way down to his gut, where it detonated. Stifling a cough, MacKinnon reached across the rickety table and brought the bottle closer. The label read Old Overholt, all right, but MacKinnon knew this bottle had not held legitimate rye whiskey in months. His eyes began to water, but he refilled the cup with more of the forty-rod. This territory would be covered with green grass three feet high from Colorado to Mexico before that miser of a barkeep got the better of Sam MacKinnon. Besides, Jace Martin was buying the whiskey. It wasn't costing MacKinnon a thing, except his liver.

"The Three of Spades Saloon is as good as a bank," Martin said. "Probably has more money in it than most banks in these parts. And there ain't a bank in Bonito City."

The saloon in which they sat had no name. It had no windows, either, but the door remained open, allowing a draft and some light to fall on the table, which was nothing more than a keg with a solid ox-cart wheel nailed to the top.

Jace Martin leaned forward. He was younger than MacKinnon, thinner, too, with bright eyes and a drooping dark mustache. Martin pushed back his black hat. "The Bonito City Mining Company will pay off its miners on Friday," Martin said softly. "They'll lose most of their wages Friday night at the Three of Spades. What they don't lose Friday, they'll lose Saturday. On Sunday morning, while every miner in town is sleeping off a drunk, Charley The Trey will put his profits on the stage to Mesilla."

"And we rob the stage." This time, MacKinnon only sipped the forty-rod.

"No. The stage has a guard, and the guard has a Greener ten-gauge, sawed off. We rob the saloon before the stage gets to town."

MacKinnon set the glass on the wheel table top. He rubbed the graying stubble on his chin. Leaning back, he studied Jace Martin seriously, instead of skeptically.

"Jace," he said, "I've swung a wide loop in my day, and I've done some work with a running iron. I've raised my share of Cain. I cheated Delmar Evans at poker, but that was Delmar Evans, and he deserved it. But robbing a person . . ."

"Charley The Trey ain't no person. His dice are loaded, his faro layout is as crooked as his roulette wheels. We rob him, and we'll be cheered as heroes by every miner in Bonito City. We'll be written up in those nickel books you fancy. Buffalo Bill Cody will want to shake our hand. The territorial governor will give us a medal."

"Or they'll be turning Charley The Trey into a Deadwood Dick." MacKinnon managed to laugh as he shook his head and refilled his glass with more of that gut-chewing concoction. "If I remember right, the graveyard at Bonito City has two or three residents, courtesy of Charley The Trey."

"Four. The last came Wednesday a week ago. My brother. He was just sixteen."

MacKinnon studied the tin cup. He didn't feel like drinking the rotgut now.

"Why me, Jace? Why come to me?"

"You know the territory."

"No better than you do."

Martin pulled a cheroot from his vest pocket, bit off an end, and found a match. "I got three boys with me. The kid, Harry Parker. Four-Eyes Sherman. And Chico Archuleta." The match flared, and came up to the smoke. When the end glowed red, Martin drew in deeply, tilted his head back, and sent a plume of smoke rising toward the *vigas*. "I'd like . . ." Martin straightened in the rickety chair and smiled across the wheel. "I'd like someone with me that I could trust."

"You think you could trust me?" MacKinnon asked.

"More than Parker, Sherman, or the Mex."

"I didn't know you had a brother." MacKinnon drank more whiskey. It didn't burn as much now.

"He wasn't much of a brother. Not worth mentioning. Just got into the territory last week."

MacKinnon studied the younger man's face. *No. He's lying to me, the territory's biggest liar. He ain't got a brother. He's trying to sucker me in. But I'm broke and tired enough to let him do it. Hell, it might even be fun, like one of them adventure stories.*

Martin flicked ash onto the dirt floor. "You ever won a dime at The Three of Spades?"

MacKinnon's head shook. "But I've only bucked the tiger there a couple of times."

"You got a job?"

He smiled. "Riding the grub line."

"Well." Martin placed the cigar on the rusted airtight that served as an ashtray. "You won't have to ride for any brand for a while after Sunday. We split six ways. Even. The sixth share goes to my mother in Akron, Ohio."

MacKinnon snorted up whiskey.

Mother. Like hell. I ought to teach Jace a few things about lying. You don't push your bull too far. But I haven't done a stupid thing in months. And Charley The Trey's the biggest jackass in the county.

No, MacKinnon now realized, *Jace Martin was a bigger ass.* If MacKinnon had not been fairly drunk at the time, and broke, and just a stupid thirty-a-month cowhand, he would have laughed in Jace Martin's face, thanked him for the whiskey, and ridden down to Seven Rivers to see if he could find work there. Only a fool would not have seen how Jace Martin was playing MacKinnon. But Sam MacKinnon had often been a fool, known to do foolish things.

That had been a failing for many a year.

"Mother," he said, spit, and gripped a tree

35

branch for support. He studied the path down, saw about a hundred rocks and dead branches that he might trip over, and looked for something he could use as a crutch. He hated the thought of using a crutch—about as much as he despised being afoot. But it wasn't like anyone could see him in these hills.

Problem was, there wasn't anything he could find to help him move.

Carefully, he put one foot ahead.

He carried on a conversation with himself. In his head. That's how he always night-herded, or passed the time riding drag on a cattle drive.

When a man has seen better than forty years pass him by, after more chuckle-headed horses than he can count, a bad shoulder, an aching back, and countless joints that needed a good oiling, he realizes that he should have done a better job of saving his wages. Remember that old cook up along the Pecos toward Glorieta Mesa? Not the Mexican, but before that. Eli. Yep. Eli was his name. Eli Radovan. Kept most of his wages in a whiskey jug he kept buried behind the privy. Everybody laughed at the old belly-cheater, but old Eli Radovan might have been smarter than any banker in the territory.

Two years back, or thereabouts. Remember? Hung my hat on the elk horn by the door and found a spot on the counter at Eli's Café by the railroad depot in Lamy. Eli wasn't even doing

36

the cooking. He just sat in a corner in his Prince Albert and a silk shirt with mother of pearl buttons. Just sat, and watched people eat. I paid fifteen cents for a steak, posole, and tortillas. With coffee, too. Eli never served grub like that over at Glorieta.

There ain't much to Lamy, but the trains stop there, and a spur carries passengers to Santa Fe. Eli's Café was doing business morning, noon, and night, and Eli Radovan tells me, after we shake hands, that he's keeping his money in two banks. Two! Didn't offer to pay for my supper, neither, that belly-cheating miser.

Maybe that's why Sam MacKinnon had talked himself into riding into Bonito City with Jace Martin that Sunday morning.

A few years back, there was no such place as Bonito City, and Bonito Cañon remained empty except for trees, deer, bears, and bobcats. The Río Bonito provided pretty good water, during wet years at least, and it wasn't hard for folks from Ruidoso or White Oaks to get to. Miners started putting up cabins, and when one of them discovered silver ore, Bonito City was born.

These days, Bonito City had three mercantiles, a halfway decent blacksmith, a hotel that also housed the post office, one lawyer, a café, a constable who would be sleeping off his Saturday drunk and long hours this morning, several shanties for miners, and quite a few lode mines, mainly the Río Bonito Mining Company. Folks had talked about building a church to go with the graveyard, and maybe even a schoolhouse to make the town respectable. Of course, there was Charley The Trey's Three of Spades Saloon. Charley The Trey did not put rot-gut whiskey in Old Overholt bottles. He imported Scotch, even French brandy. Charged San Francisco prices, too.

A man who raked in that much money, and who still had his gamblers cheat, could afford to lose some money, MacKinnon reasoned.

At the livery stable on the edge of town, the five riders reined up. They fished wheat sacks from their saddlebags, removed their hats, and slipped the coarse material over their heads. Four-Eyes Sherman eased the spectacles from the bridge of his nose, folded the earpieces, and carefully placed the eyeglasses in the pocket of his shirtfront, which he buttoned for safekeeping. MacKinnon studied the wheat sack before slipping it over his own head. Holes had been cut out for the eyes, so MacKinnon adjusted his and breathed in ground wheat. He let his hat fall behind his back, secured with a rawhide string that he positioned underneath the tied ends of his frayed bandanna. That would help keep the rawhide from choking him if he had to put his mare into a hard lope on the way out of town.

The stagecoach was scheduled to arrive at seven-fifteen. Jace Martin pulled the heavy watch out of his vest pocket, smiled, and slipped the watch out of sight. "Should be just a few more . . ." He stopped, and stood in the stirrups. A door had opened, closed. Footsteps sounded on the boardwalk, then stopped. "Let's start the ball, boys," Martin said. The wheat sack also masked his voice.

Drawing revolvers from their holsters, the five men turned their horses, spurred them hard, and rounded the livery, churning sod as they galloped down Bonito City's main street.

Charley The Trey's saloon stood between two vacant lots on the west side of the street. The lot between the saloon and the hotel served as sort of a pen for the change of teams for the stagecoach. Charley The Trey had stopped in the lot, talking to the old-timer who always helped change the team for the stage. A pair of saddlebags hung over Charley's left shoulder. The cheating saloonkeeper must have thought the hoof beats meant the stagecoach was pulling in a few minutes early, because he just kept talking to the old coot with the four mules.

When Charley The Trey looked up, he straightened and reached for the pistol he wore butt forward on his left hip.

By then he was too late, and he knew it.

MacKinnon reined up his sorrel mare, and leveled the Remington .44 at Charley The Trey's nose. MacKinnon's mouth opened, but no words came out. He couldn't think of what to say.

"Don't say a word!" Martin swung out of his saddle. "Run those mules off."

Harry Parker, the kid, eased his gelding toward the bald-headed old man and the mules.

Martin jerked the nickel-plated Schofield from Charley The Trey's holster, and pitched it into the street. Chuckling, Martin removed the saddlebags off the gambler's shoulder.

"Heavy," Martin said. "More than I expected. Must have been better than a normal weekend for you."

Quit talking, MacKinnon thought as he ground his teeth. The Remington felt like a mountain howitzer in his hand. His breathing became ragged, and he felt himself sweating underneath the choking, floury smelling wheat sack. He cursed himself for a coward. Next to Four-Eyes Sherman, MacKinnon was the oldest man riding with Jace Martin. And acting greener than Harry Parker.

He felt that way until Harry Parker started shooting his pistol in the air.

The sorrel bucked at the rapid gunfire that sent echoes bouncing back and forth along Bonito Cañon. MacKinnon tightened his legs against the mare's sides. His left hand gripped the reins like a vice, and his right hand reached for the saddle horn. He saw the Remington falling to the ground at Charley The Trey's feet.

MacKinnon swore as he tried to get control of Honey, his sorrel.

She was a sweet horse. Eight years old. Loved apples. Never complained. Had an easy gait. Even her trot wouldn't break an old man's backbone. She could cut cattle with the best Texas gelding. Honey never bucked.

Till this morning.

Eight jumps later, he had Honey under control. He wanted to spur her, run her hard up and down the town's main road, Bonito City's only road that was little more than a mule trace or footpath. Teach her a lesson.

As MacKinnon managed to turn Honey around, he saw four, five, maybe six men tumbling out of the front door to the hotel. Across the street, more men came out of the café. Down the street, a man with long dark hair and a big black hat stepped from the livery stable.

Jace Martin's plan was fraying.

One of the men in front of the café pushed back his jacket.

"Robbery!" he shouted, and MacKinnon caught a glimpse of something pinned on the lapel of the man's checked vest.

This wasn't Bonito City's constable. The constable was an old man with spectacles who

41

carried a single-shot shotgun that he kept loaded with birdshot, not buckshot.

The man with the badge bore a striking resemblance to Nelson Bookbinder, sheriff of Lincoln County. MacKinnon had once heard him give a speech in Tularosa. And he had read three of the books written about him by that Colonel What's-His-Name at a line shack on the Plains of San Agustin.

A bullet sang past MacKinnon's nose. He leaned in the saddle, saw Charley The Trey rolling on the grass between his saloon and the hotel. The mules ran toward the river, and the old stock tender chased after them on bowed legs.

Jace Martin threw the saddlebags in front of his saddle before he climbed aboard his buckskin.

Four-Eyes Sherman fired three shots at the men in front of the café. The men dived this way and that, except for the one who had almost shot off MacKinnon's nose. That man barely moved, didn't blink or shudder, just moved his arm, thumb, and finger. The pistol roared. Four-Eyes Sherman swore, and swung his horse toward the hotel and livery.

"Not that way!" MacKinnon yelled. "The stage. We'll meet the stage!"

The kid Parker tried to climb into his saddle, but his horse kept kicking and bucking. Chico Archuleta fired two shots at the men by the hotel, and spurred his gelding across the empty lot.

Jace Martin raced right behind him. MacKinnon kicked the sorrel into a lope. Honey needed little urging, but he reined her to a sliding stop when he came to Parker. Four-Eyes Sherman thundered past. MacKinnon leaned forward till his fingers slipped into the headstall on Parker's horse. A bullet whistled over MacKinnon's shoulder. Parker's horse twisted, turned, but MacKinnon kept his grip, and—after a bullet whined off a rock in front of them—the kid managed to climb halfway into the saddle. Which was enough for MacKinnon. He released his grip, and watched the horse thunder across the lot. Parker somehow managed not to fall and somehow swung his right leg over the saddle at a lope. The horse rounded the rear of the saloon, and MacKinnon felt a bullet clip his collar before Honey carried him behind the log building. More bullets thudded into the logs.

The three others were a good fifty yards ahead of MacKinnon and Parker. The trio did not show any intention of waiting for the two to catch up. They just rode. They did not even remove the wheat sacks from their heads.

Chapter Four

The five men did not stop until they reached the road to La Iglesia de San Patricio, and they did not rest there for long.

"What the Sam Hill were you doing, boy?" Jace Martin snapped at Parker after whipping off the wheat sack and dropping it on the road.

"Chasing off the mules," the kid stammered. He had trouble getting the sack off his face. He had also lost his hat.

The hats belonging to the others, including Sam MacKinnon, had been saved by stampede strings. MacKinnon let his sack fall to the ground, and he pulled the hat from his back and shoved it on his sweaty hair. The uncovered faces of the men were wet with sweat and stained here and there with traces of flour.

"Which way?" Four-Eyes Sherman asked.

"Not on this road," Martin said. "We'd be easy targets." His horse wanted to keep running, and Martin had trouble keeping him under control. He pointed at the forested hills on the other side of the road. "That way!"

"There ain't no path," Sherman said.

"Exactly."

• • •

They should have stuck to the road.

Climbing up, down, around, ducking underneath branches, squeezing between towering trees, making poor time. At some places, they had to dismount and pull skittish horses across rugged terrain.

They reached what passed for a clearing. MacKinnon waved his hands to chase away the bugs. His clothes were wet with sweat, and the air cooled him. The four others appeared in equally wretched condition.

Parker reached for his canteen. MacKinnon twisted in the saddle and stared down the mountainside.

"What is it?" Jace Martin did not sound calm.

"They're behind us," MacKinnon said.

"They cannot be," Chico Archuleta said.

"They are," MacKinnon insisted.

The men fell silent, but kept breathing in deeply, struggling for breath. Their horses labored just as hard.

Metal hoofs on hard stone. Snapping branches. A rock tumbling. A man's curse.

Jace Martin swore softly, and pulled his black hat lower and tighter on his head. He studied MacKinnon and asked: "What happened to your revolver?"

MacKinnon's right hand dropped toward the holster on his right hip. Sure enough, it was empty. Then he remembered the kid's cannonade to frighten the mules had sent Honey into a bucking fit. "Dropped it," he said, "during the ruction."

"You might need it if we sit here much longer," Four-Eyes Sherman said.

"I've got my long gun." Still, MacKinnon shot a glance at the scabbard just to make sure. For all he could recall, he had lost the Winchester, too.

"Let's go," Martin said, and they continued to climb, to descend, to twist and turn.

The pistol left in Bonito City wasn't much, MacKinnon told himself. An old Remington .44, cap-and-ball, from the Civil War era that had been converted to take brass cartridges. Sam MacKinnon had used it more often as a hammer than as a weapon. In fact, he could count the times he had pulled its trigger, and couldn't remember the last time he had even cleaned it. It had not occurred to him even to check the loads before riding into Bonito City that morning. Like most cowhands, the pistol usually came out of its holster to drive a nail or tack into a barn wall, a bunkhouse, a privy, or, Lord forbid, a fence post.

As they rode up the mountain, he remembered something else about the old piece of iron. When he had first bought the revolver, he had taken a knife and scratched his initials in the metal underneath the handle. That had been so long ago, though, he doubted if anyone could make out the crudely carved **SM**, but that had not been enough for a young cowboy with a revolver. So he had carved those initials into the walnut grips, and those had been deep, easy for anyone to see.

He tried to think how many men in Bonito City might know him, and who could identify an old Remington conversion as belonging to Sam MacKinnon.

Nobody knows me in Bonito City. And I had a sack over my face. Even without that mask, Nelson Bookbinder won't know me from Adam's off ox. No. And maybe that wasn't Bookbinder. Just my imagination. Yeah. Bookbinder wouldn't have no call to be in Bonito City. Charley The Trey saw me eighteen months ago, and I lost money. He's got no reason to remember some sucker who lost money. And . . . was that an Indian I saw? Wearing a black hat? Maybe Bookbinder's Apache? No. No. Don't get yourself worked up. Aw, Sam MacKinnon, you done put yourself where you don't want to be.

They came to what served as a bridge across a sharp drop to their left, and a shorter fall to the right. The birds had stopped singing, but the limbs of trees rustled above them. In some places you could make out the sky. In other spots, there was little to see except granite and green.

Twisting in the saddle, MacKinnon listened.

Was that the sound of revolvers being cocked, and ejection rods shoving out empty brass casings? Then a sound like a cork being popped out of a canteen. MacKinnon leaned forward, and his eyes searched through the trees and rocks. Jace Martin moved his horse beside MacKinnon.

"Well?" Martin asked.

"They sound closer," MacKinnon said.

"They can't be!" Archuleta said.

"Shut up, Chico." Jace Martin held his revolver in his right hand.

"When do we get off this mountain?" Four-Eyes Sherman asked.

"Another rise," Martin said, "then we'll swing down. East. Make for Roswell. They'll think we're headed for Mexico. We'll move for Texas."

"That country's the worst you'll find in the territory," Chico Archuleta said.

"Yeah. And it's hard to follow a trail across that wasteland." Martin smiled at MacKinnon. "What do you think?"

"They might give up, but . . ." MacKinnon sighed and stared at Martin. "I thought I saw Nelson Bookbinder and his Mescalero manhunter back there."

Martin paled. "You're joking."

MacKinnon shrugged. "I hope I'm wrong."

Martin looked down the mountain. "Charley

48

The Trey will likely put up a reward," he said.

"It'd take a mighty big bankroll for a man to chase anyone through that country," MacKinnon said. "They wouldn't pull in that much money in Bonito City." He looked back down the trail. "They're coming, whoever they are. Maybe it was just my imagination. I hope so. I'd rather deal with Charley The Trey than . . ." He let the names trail off.

"Cinch up, boys," Martin said. "We probably won't have time to stop for a while."

MacKinnon was already slipping to the ground. He shoved the stirrup up, and began working the cinch.

"Of course," Martin said with a smirk, "if we left someone behind, that might slake their thirst. Give them someone to arrest. Or hang."

MacKinnon looked up. He saw that glint in Jace Martin's eyes, and MacKinnon's right hand dashed for the Remington that had been lost in Bonito City. Martin leaned forward, and slammed the barrel of his revolver across MacKinnon's head. Honey reared, whinnied, and MacKinnon thought he saw Jace Martin fighting to right himself in his saddle, to keep his horse from backing off the edge. But it was hard to tell, because MacKinnon lay on his back, his head throbbing, blood and sweat mingling, dripping, burning his eyes. He heard Honey's hoofs as the horse started to turn toward him. He hit a rock,

49

rolled over saplings, felt the earth moving with him as he slid, rolling and toppling. The horse kicked a small avalanche after him as MacKinnon kept tumbling down.

"Ride, boys, ride!" Jace Martin shouted.

MacKinnon landed hard against a rock. He turned, and saw Honey somersaulting her way down the slope toward him. An eight-hundred-pound mare would crush him, so MacKinnon dived again. He dropped another six or seven feet, and this time his right side smashed against a boulder.

Honey kept coming down the embankment though. Despite the pain in MacKinnon's side, his head, his whole forty-and-more-year-old body, he came to his knees and staggered four or five more feet before he collapsed.

The earth stopped moving. He tasted dust, sweat, and blood. He heard Honey scream, come to her feet, and bolt. Which way? He wasn't sure.

For a minute, he lay there, breathing hard, each breath causing him to shudder. His left hand clutched his ribs. Blood flooded his right eye.

He was alive. That much he knew. He heard a voice, and he knew that if he lay here, he would be caught, maybe lynched. Sitting up almost killed him. Down the ridge, a few yards to his left, he saw a massive boulder, and a fallen log.

It wasn't much of a hiding place, but MacKinnon could see nothing better.

All he had to figure out was how he could cross those ten yards.

But he made it.

Now, after an agonizing eternity spent hiding and sweating, MacKinnon found himself alone in the mountains. But he remembered Jace Martin, who had betrayed him. That started him walking, somehow.

Only not for long.

His feet shot out from under him. Landing hard on his buttocks, he slid down the embankment—before he could cry out in pain or curse his luck—kicking up stones and dirt, till he came to a stop.

MacKinnon cradled his ribs, eased over onto his side, and waited till he didn't hurt so much.

He coughed, and finally chuckled.

"That was," he said in a dry whisper, "faster than walking."

Chapter Five

Honey had loped off this way, which was not why he had started walking—hobbling would be a better choice of words—in this direction. Nelson Bookbinder and his posse had ridden off the opposite way. So had Jace Martin, that Judas, and his three followers. If Charley The Trey came up this mountain with his own group of gunmen, they would be far up the ridge and unlikely to hear him. He followed a deer trail through the forest and the rocks. Eventually, he might even hit the road.

Then what?

He answered his own question. *Don't get ahead of yourself, MacKinnon. Focus on the job at hand. Right foot. Left foot. Right foot. Left foot. Stop here. Grip that young Douglas fir and wait here till you catch your breath.*

How cold would it get after sunset? He turned and lifted his head. The treetops stretched up toward the sky, which might have started darkening, but he couldn't really tell. He didn't feel any cooler right now. His ribs hurt. His head throbbed, but not as painfully as earlier, and at least the gash above his right eye had stopped bleeding.

The hat came off, and MacKinnon wiped his

brow, carefully maneuvering around the cut, and he wet his lips again and studied the countryside.

He just stood there, sore, dazed, and pretty much lost, for maybe five minutes, possibly fifteen, perhaps as long as an hour.

That's when he heard the noise.

MacKinnon blinked. Had he imagined it? He turned and looked down the rock-rimmed ridge. Bear? No, bears did not come with saddles and bridles, and he had never seen a sorrel-colored bear.

"Honey," he said, and repeated the name louder, but not so loud that anyone along the ridge could hear.

The mare stopped scratching her hide against a tree, and lifted her head. She whinnied, and started pawing the rocks.

MacKinnon moved away from the sapling. A while back, he had found a stick that served as a crutch, and this helped him ease his way down without breaking more ribs, or his neck.

The mare did not move, did not run, and MacKinnon gathered up the reins, and began rubbing Honey's neck with the flat of his hand in a circular motion. "That's a good girl," he told the horse. "Where'd you run off to, Honey? Miss me?" He shook his head. "I sure missed you."

He found the canteen, surprised that it had survived the tumble down the mountainside or Honey's lope through the forest. He brushed pine needles and bark off the saddle, saddlebags, his bedroll, and from the reddish coat tied behind the cantle. He tried to remove the canteen. Tried harder. Cursed, and began working on the knot.

"No wonder this didn't come off," he said. For a moment, MacKinnon thought that he might have to break out the pocket knife and cut the straps. But at last he solved the puzzle, and brought up the canteen, shaking it, and hearing the reassuring sound of water sloshing. After unscrewing the cap, he lifted the canteen with both hands, ignored the pain that sliced through his ribs, and drank long. He stopped, wiped his mouth, and almost brought the canteen up again. This time, he stopped.

He removed his hat, laid it crown-down on the rocks, and partly filled it with water. He let Honey drink as he moved around her, staying close to her body, and checking for injuries. He found scratches, along with more rubble from the mountainside. He checked her legs, the iron shoes, her feet, her withers, and ran his hands underneath the saddle blanket. She needed a good brushing and some healthy work with a currycomb, but she should be able to carry him— after he straightened and cinched the saddle. If he could manage to do that.

He splashed more water in the hat, took a final swallow for himself, and wrapped the strap around the horn. He still couldn't figure out how that knot had formed, but chalked it up to the roll down the drop-off. He opened one of the saddlebags and reached for the bottle of whiskey.

He pulled out the neck, which still held the cork, but there was nothing else but shards of busted glass.

"Can't have everything." He tossed the trash against a tree trunk. He would have to empty the rest of the busted glass later. MacKinnon went back around Honey and opened the other bag. First he found a stupid dime novel about Kit Carson, which he pitched to the ground. Next he pulled out a leather purse, and he tugged on the rawhide thongs to loosen the opening. He brought out a piece of jerky and devoured it. He pulled out a larger pouch, and dumped oats on the ground for the horse.

Picking up his hat left him hugging his ribs, and putting the battered old thing on his head hurt just as much, but the wetness of the fur felt revived him.

As the mare kept eating, MacKinnon drew the Winchester from its scabbard. The carbine was an 1873 model in .38-40 caliber, twenty-inch barrel, not fancy, pretty battered up from the years MacKinnon had owned it and even more scratched and nicked after Honey's lope through these woods and rocks. He carefully worked the lever just enough to make sure he still had a cartridge in the chamber. After brushing off the straw and dust, he slipped the carbine back into the scabbard and unbuckled his belt and holster. The gun rig might be enough for a judge and jury—and certainly more than enough for Charley The Trey or even Sheriff Nelson Bookbinder—to convict him of the saloon robbery.

If he happened to get caught.

MacKinnon had no intention of getting caught. At least, not until he met up with Jace Martin.

Belt and holster fell to the ground.

Honey had finished eating, so MacKinnon shoved the saddle to its proper position and cinched it tight.

That took about all he had, and he squatted by the horse for a few minutes, and used the stirrup to help pull himself back to his feet. Which left him gasping for breath.

His horse stared at him. "You ready?" MacKinnon said to the mare, and answered for himself. "I ain't."

After leading the sorrel from the rocks and the trees, he found a spot that seemed high enough for his needs. He kept Honey on the low ground, lifted his foot into the stirrup from the high spot, paused, grimaced, and swung into the saddle.

That hurt enough that he waited a moment before sliding his right boot into the other stirrup.

"All right," he said after he could breathe again. "You pick a path, girl. You've seen more of this mountain than I have."

• • •

His mistake had been thinking that riding horse-back wouldn't persecute his ribs. He had not counted on all the ducking he would have to do underneath branches, or all the leaning to one side or the other to avoid trees and boulders. Honey picked paths down loose rocks, up steep ridges, and over fallen timbers.

MacKinnon often leaned over, wondering if he would vomit. He came to places where any sane man would have dismounted to walk alongside his horse up or down or around or between. Yet he couldn't climb out of the saddle, because the blinding pain in his side convinced him that once he was out of the saddle, he'd never be able to pull himself into it again.

He rode. He weaved from one side to another. He couldn't even carry on a conversation with himself. He just rode.

Slowly, MacKinnon began to feel less enclosed. The air felt cleaner. The sky, even though the sun had started sinking behind the mountains, seemed brighter.

Straightening, he realized that they had reached a clearing. He recognized the sound of splashing water. Honey stopped, lowered her head, and began to drink. Glancing down, MacKinnon was surprised to see the water. Honey had found a small pond, or lake, from snow melt, or maybe it was a beaver pond. He didn't care. He dropped the reins over the sorrel's neck, and pulled the canteen close to him.

Still, he couldn't dismount, no matter how the water beckoned him. He unscrewed the canteen's cap, and leaned low, dropping the canteen in the water—but only after wrapping the canvas straps twice over his right hand.

He dragged the canteen toward his mare's head, and pulled it back toward her tail. Back and forth. The container grew heavier. He kept at it.

This is harder than it looked, he thought.

The canteen was made of wood, and lined on the inside with beeswax. Wood floated, and the canteen had been practically empty. He kept trying, though, and when Honey started to walk, MacKinnon grabbed the reins with his left hand and pulled her up short. *Maybe,* he thought, *I should just let Honey walk through the water and let the canteen drag behind.*

It helped. He reined Honey to a stop and pulled the canteen out of the pond. He drank.

Honey snorted.

"You had yours," he said. "My turn."

He shook the canteen. He sighed. Maybe a quarter full, and by now darkness was coming quickly. He turned Honey to cross the pond again, dragging the canteen, feeling it become heavier and heavier as it sank deeper under the clear, cool water. Honey stopped again, and this time MacKinnon felt the horse's movement.

"No." He straightened, and brought the reins up short. *You ain't rolling. A bath comes later.* He kicked the mare's ribs, cursed her, urged her out of the pond. Horses like to roll in the water, and MacKinnon had laughed at cowboys, experienced and greenhorns alike, who had been caught unexpectedly and wound up soaking wet while their mounts rolled in some pond or river.

When he stopped the horse on dry land, MacKinnon's ribs blazed with pain. He bit his lips, and remembered his canteen. It wasn't quite full, but it would have to do. He took another sip, screwed the lid on tight, and wrapped the straps around the horn. Horse and rider moved back into the hills and trees.

A few minutes later, the darkness of night covered them like a shroud.

CHAPTER SIX

Katie Callahan stepped out from the hole she had managed to scratch out thus far, and began massaging her head. It felt like someone had been driving twelve-penny nails into her temples. Her eyes closed as she squatted, and she felt the wind cool her, but only slightly.

When she looked again at what she had dug, she sighed. Deeper, maybe, but not deep enough for even the body of a woman ravaged by consumption and too many miles of hard traveling from one mining camp to another. It might have to do. She wouldn't be able to do much more now that the sun had begun to sink and, over by the broken wagon wheel, Gary kept kicking a baseball, and mumbling: "I'm hungry."

She rose, her knees stiff and her hands and shoulders throbbing, and moved to the barrel on the side of the wagon.

When she opened the lid, Gary changed his tune. He even stopped booting the dirty, old ball. "I'm thirsty, Katie," he said.

After finding the ladle, Katie had to strain to reach the water. "I thought . . ." She didn't recognize her voice. It was if it wasn't hers. That dry, ragged sound belonged to one of those cigarette-smoking strumpets in Chloride . . . Vera

Cruz . . . "I thought," she tried again, bringing the ladle up, "that you were hungry."

"I'm thirsty, too."

She nodded, motioned with her head, and he came quickly to her. She let him drink.

Why not? she thought. Seeing him drink, watching him revive with just that little bit of water, made her smile, but smiling hurt her lips. He grinned as he handed her the ladle, and she dipped it again into the barrel and brought it up, emptied about half of it, and drank what was left.

Gary gathered bits of dead cactus spines, dried brush, and blew softly on the tinder once Katie had managed to get that lighted. He did not always act like a stupid, lazy, kid brother.

Gary could learn, too, and pretty quickly. She didn't have to remind him to let the small pieces catch first, let them burn hot, before slowly adding more wood to the fire. Once they had the fire going, she moved to the front of the wagon, climbed on the wheel's cap, and reached onto the driver's bench for the skillet and the sack of salt pork.

"Can we have something good to eat?" Gary asked.

"We have what we have," Katie told him, adding softly, "and not much left of that."

"If you'd let me go hunting," Gary suggested, one more time.

"That shotgun's bigger than you," she said.

"I can shoot."

"Don't you touch that shotgun, Gary. Don't even think about it."

"You ain't my ma," Gary said. "You don't boss me. I'm telling Ma."

"Shut up," Katie snapped.

When she had the skillet on the coals, and the salt pork had started to sizzle, she fetched the kettle, and ladled enough water to cover the used tea leaves so that the three of them could have something to wash down the meat and soften the hardtack. There would be no more hardtack after tonight. Katie wouldn't be saddened by that.

"It smells yummy," Gary said.

Katie stared at him.

"It does," he insisted.

She turned toward the wagon. "Go fetch Florrie," she told him.

"And Ma?"

Katie squeezed her eyes shut. "Just . . . Florrie."

Gary rose, kicked the baseball toward the busted wheel, and moved to the back of the wagon, as Katie arranged the cups and began to fill the three containers with weak, flavorless tea.

"Florrie says she ain't hungry," Gary called out.

Katie tried to rein in her temper. "Tell her that she has to eat."

Setting the kettle, now empty, in the sand, she

speared a hunk of salt pork and placed it on one plate near three hardtack crackers.

"She won't come," Gary announced.

She jabbed the knife into the next piece of meat and yelled: "Florrie, get out of that wagon and put your behind by this fire now! Before I drag you out by your red hair!"

After practically throwing the last piece of pork onto the last plate, she grabbed the skillet's handle and, cursing, pulled back, shaking her burning hand. She found Truluck's old work glove at her knees, but did not bother pulling it on, just used it to lift the skillet off the coals and dropped it on a flat rock. Grease slopped over the sides, and some spilled onto the coals, igniting a small, brief flame.

Katie bit her lip. She turned toward the wagon. Gary stood by the tailgate, eyes wide, mouth open. Florrie climbed out of the wagon, glared at Gary, looked at Katie as though she were staring at the devil. Florrie snatched Gary's little hand and practically dragged him toward the fire, the plates, the cups, and what would have to pass for supper.

Florrie offered no apology. Neither did Katie. As soon as Florrie released her hold on Gary's hand, he forgot all about the abuse, squatted by the fire, and picked up his plate. Katie realized she had forgotten to bring any utensils except for the knife she had used on the salt pork.

She softened her voice. "Dip the crackers in the tea," she instructed Gary. "It'll soften them so you won't break your teeth."

Florrie looked for a fork and, finding none, glared at Katie, who picked up the salt pork with her fingers and began eating. It was tough, burned, and, after two days of eating nothing but salt pork and hardtack, rather sickening. She tore off a hunk, like some wolf, dropped the rest on the tin plate, and wiped her fingers on her skirt. She wiped too hard, forgetting about the blisters and embedded slivers on her hands from digging.

"Ohhh!" Gary sang out. "There's worms in my crackers."

Closing her eyes, Katie wished she were dead. Then she thought about her mother, still lying in the back of the wagon. When she opened her eyes, she found Florrie pitching the hardtack off her plate and into the fire. That excited Gary, who did the same.

"Burn," he said. "Burn, worms, burn."

"Is this all we have?" Florrie asked.

"Eat the pork," Katie said. "Drink the tea."

"Shouldn't we bring some supper to Ma?" Gary said.

"Ma's dead!" Florrie shrieked.

Gary burst into tears.

Satan snatched Katie's soul. "What the hell, Florrie!"

"Shut up. Shut up. Shut up!" her sister cried.

"She's dead. Dead. Dead. Dead. What are you going to do . . . just keep her in the back of the wagon till the buzzards come?"

"I'm digging a grave!"

"That's not a grave, Sister."

"Well, maybe if you'd climb out of that wagon and just help me!"

"That's Mother! That's my mother! And she's dead. And we're all going to be dead . . . just like her."

"Shut up!"

"I won't shut up!"

"Shut up!"

"No."

Katie slapped her sister. But not just once. She slapped her with her right hand, then her left, then again, and again, and again, ignoring the blisters, the splinters, the rawness of her palms. She stopped once she realized the slaps were only making Gary wail harder. Florrie lay curled up into a ball, and she remembered how many times Tommy Truluck had beaten her, when she was younger, and Florrie, Gary . . . even Ma.

Slaps would not bring back their mother. They wouldn't help them get out of this kiln.

Florrie sobbed. Gary bawled. Katie had nothing left inside her. She was as empty as this desert.

Sighing, she slid over to her sobbing brother. She put her arm around the child, and pulled him close. She reached for Florrie, but her sister rolled away, dumped her supper on the sand, and stormed off several yards from the fire and the wagon. She just stood in the darkness, staring at the big empty.

Keep walking, Katie thought. *Go on. Just go. What have you done to help . . . ?*

She made herself stop, despising herself for such thoughts. Bringing her hand down under Gary's chin, she lifted his head. She did her best to smile, and wet her lips, before saying: "It's all right, Gary." Though it was anything but *all right.*

"Ma . . . ? She . . . she ain't . . . dead . . . is she?" Gary whimpered.

Katie sighed. She thought she would have to blink away tears, but there were no tears. "Yes, sweetie, I'm afraid she is." She pulled Gary closer, and hugged him tightly.

"But . . . she can't be. . . ."

Letting him cry a while, she tried to think of something to say, but there was nothing to say.

"I guess I knew she was dead."

Katie looked down at Gary. He had stopped crying. She looked over the coals and into the desert night and saw Florrie, no longer standing, but sitting on her knees, tossing stones into the darkness.

"Why did Ma have to die?" Gary asked.

She brought him closer. "She was just played out, Gary. She lasted longer than anyone thought she would. She was sick before you were born. She was sick as long as I can remember."

"Could Pa have saved her?"

"No." She said it too quickly, but then the honesty of her answer struck her. "Nobody could have saved her. She was sick. Sometimes sick people get better. Sometimes." She lifted her head toward the stars. "Sometimes . . . well . . . she's in heaven. She's not sick anymore."

"I bet Pa could've saved her."

She let go, and tried to get feeling back in her arms and legs. "Maybe," she said bitterly. She thought: *He could have stayed to help me dig a grave.*

"I don't want Ma to be dead," Gary said, and started sobbing into Katie's blouse.

"I don't either, Gary," she said, pulling him close. "But . . ."

Nudging her sleeping brother, Katie waited for his eyes to open. He raised his head toward her.

"The coals are dying," she said. "Want to help me put some more wood on them?"

"All right." He yawned.

Gary walked on his knees to the fire, and Katie tried moving her arm, which had fallen asleep. She could see the prostrate form of Florrie at the edge of the camp. Her sister had fallen asleep, too. The moon would soon rise. The mule brayed.

Swearing softly, she made herself stand, but had to wait for feeling to return to her legs before she could walk to the water barrel. She had not given the mule any water since this morning. How could she be so stupid?

"Little sticks first," she reminded Gary. She opened the lid, found the ladle, and filled a tin bowl with water. "That's fine," she told her brother, and set the bowl in front of Bartholomew. She stroked his mane as he bent wearily and began to drink. Should she give him more? Her eyes squeezed shut for the millionth time.

I am nineteen years old, she thought to herself. *I should be on my own by now. Not playing nursemaid to a kid sister and a stepbrother. Not being an undertaker. Not being stranded in the middle of Hades with no luck, no future, no hope . . .*

No chance.

She stopped. She could have, should have, struck out on her own years ago. But then who would have looked after Ma . . . after Florrie and Gary? Tommy Truluck? Not hardly. So Katie had sacrificed her future for her family. She'd be an old maid . . . if she didn't die in this desert. This, she kept reminding herself, got her nowhere. She let the mule drink, and returned to the fire, which Gary had flaming again.

"Florrie!" she called out.

"Let me go," Gary said. "I'll kick her till she wakes up."

"Feed the fire," she said, and called Florrie's name again.

The figure moved, rose off the ground, looked one way, then at the fire.

"Come on. We all need some sleep," Katie said.

But where?

Florrie was walking groggily, in no particular hurry, but at least coming back to camp. Florrie stumbled, stopped, turned, cursed, and bent. As she straightened, she hurled something into the darkness. Katie heard the *thunk*.

Florrie said: "Stupid rock."

That gave Katie the idea.

Chapter Seven

Florrie called the idea stupid.

"Well, what do you think we should do?" Katie spat out the words. She closed her mouth tightly. Her head had filled with blood and venom, and she could feel it about to explode. Her fingers and wrists began to throb, and she realized she had them clenched so tightly they shook.

"We bury her," Florrie said.

"That's what we'll be doing," Katie managed to say without spitting out froth or more curses.

"You're talking about covering her with rocks. That's not how you bury people."

Katie shook her head in disgust. How many rock-covered graves had they seen in towns like White Oaks and Chloride? She said as much, and when Florrie rolled her eyes, Katie painfully balled her hands into fists again.

"They cover the graves with stones after they've buried the dead six feet under." Florrie's tone sounded like that schoolteacher, Hazel Ebenezer, they'd tolerated back in Silver City.

"You see that!" Katie pointed at the shallow trench just beyond the mule and wagon. "That's what I've managed to dig all day."

"Maybe if you were stronger."

"Maybe if you'd help me."

"I'm looking after Ma."

"Ma's dead!"

"Stop yelling!" Gary wailed.

Katie spit in the fire, scooped the boy up into her arms, and brought him to her shoulder. She didn't know how she managed that. As she weakened, Gary seemed to be getting bigger and heavier, and a million pins pricked her hands and fingers.

"It's all right," she whispered. She kissed his sweaty, dirty neck. "It's all right."

"Don't fight with Florrie," he sobbed.

She glared at her sister. "It's bedrock," she told Florrie. "Even if you helped, we couldn't get much deeper."

"We take her to town," Florrie said. "To a real cemetery. Have a real preacher read over her. Folks could sing a hymn. We could put a cross . . . no, a real tombstone, made of marble . . . over her grave with everything on it. Even an angel. I've seen tombstones like that, bigger than monuments. Her name. That'll be on it, too. She was born in Eighteen Forty-Two."

"In March," Gary said. "Same as me."

"But not the same day," Florrie said. She even smiled.

"How do we get her to a town, Florrie?" Katie tried to sound patient.

Florrie turned and started to point at the wagon, sighed, and looked at the mule.

"Is that what you want, Florrie?" Now it became Katie's turn to sound like Miss Ebenezer, or as the kids in Silver City had dubbed her, Witchhazel. "Throw Ma over Bartholomew like a bedroll? We don't even know how far it is to Roswell."

"There was that church we passed west of here," Florrie said.

"Ma said it was pretty," Gary sobbed. "It had a pretty name."

"La Iglesia de San Patricio," Florrie said. Only Katie's kid sister could whisper a name and make it sound like she was singing a hymn.

Katie shifted Gary's weight. "It was a Catholic church," Katie said. "With a Catholic cemetery. Ma was . . . we are . . . Presbyterian."

"It's a church," Florrie said.

"I don't think they would let us. . . ." She sighed, and set Gary back on the ground. "We'd still have to get her there."

"Bartholomew," Florrie said. "We can make one of those . . . um . . . um . . . I can't . . . It begins with a T."

"Travois," Katie said.

"Yeah."

A hollow chuckle came out of her throat and mouth, and Katie looked at the mule, and the wagon. "So we drag Ma to that little church or to Roswell."

Florrie said, "What choice do we have?"

"And the water?" Katie asked sharply. "The only thing we have to carry water in, thanks to that black-hearted bas- . . ." Biting her bottom lip, she looked away from Gary, and stared across the dark, empty land. "A tea kettle, a coffee pot, and some cups. Do we load those with Ma's body on the travois, too? I don't know how to rig a pack saddle out of what we have that we could strap on Bartholomew's back. I don't know if that old mule's strong enough to carry that load."

"We can fix the wagon," Gary said. "I bet I could fix it."

She made herself smile, and tousled the boy's hair. "I bet you could, Gary," she said. "But even if we got the wagon fixed, Bartholomew couldn't pull it alone. It's too big. He's too small. And he's as tired as all of us. Maybe even more so. He's worked hard."

The wind picked up. The flames in the fire pit danced.

"Someone's bound to come." There was little hope in Florrie's voice, though.

"We've been here two days," Katie reminded her. She grimaced, remembering the family in the buckboard that had stopped on the first day, before Tommy Truluck abandoned them. The old man with the beard like Abe Lincoln's had asked if they wanted any help, and Tommy Truluck, who had been drinking from that stoneware jug of his, had cursed them and run them off.

"It will be hot tomorrow, too," Katie said.

She did not have to explain what she meant. Florrie wiped her eyes, sniffed, and stared at her shoes. "Ma . . ."

"Ma never cared for fancy funerals," Katie told her. "She said it wasn't how many people came to see you off, wasn't even how many people remembered you, it was *how* they remembered you."

Her sister lifted her head. "She also said funerals weren't for the dead, but for the living."

"Exactly," Katie said.

She hadn't realized how hard it would be to get her mother's body out of the wagon. Margaret Anne Roberts Callahan Truluck had always been frail, thin, weak, but in death she had become nothing but deadweight. The back of the wagon felt cramped enough—not that they ever owned much—and all Gary did in trying to help was get in the way of Katie and Florrie.

Somehow they managed to bring the blanket-wrapped body to the back of the wagon. Gary climbed down, they opened the tailgate, and Katie stepped onto the ground. She took the feet end, Florrie lifted the head-and-shoulders part, and Katie backed up till Florrie told her to stop. The redhead gently settled the torso on the gate, climbed to the ground, and caught her breath.

"Do you want to switch places?" Katie asked.

"I'll be all right," Florrie said.

"Shouldn't we wait till morning?" Gary said. "It's dark now. Real dark."

"It'll be hot in the morning," Florrie told him. "And hotter carrying rocks. We'll need a lot of rocks."

Maybe this isn't such a good idea. Katie shook her head at the thought.

Florrie gripped the woolen fabric and gave Katie a terse nod.

"Can I help?" Gary asked.

"Walk ahead of me," Katie told him. "I won't be able to see. You tell me where I'm going and don't let me step into the fire."

Now that they were out of the claustrophobic wagon, the bundle felt lighter. Katie kept backing up, relying more on Florrie than her kid brother. They passed the fire, the busted wheel, the front wheel, the wagon tongue to which Bartholomew was tethered. The mule pulled back, his ears signaling his fear, and brayed loudly. The rope strained. The girls stopped.

"Easy, boy," Katie said. "Easy. Eaaaa-sy, Bartholomew. It's all right."

"Animals can smell death," Gary said. "Pa told me."

"Gary," Katie said, "ease up to Bartholomew. Let him know he's all right. Don't get behind him. Just take hold of the rope with one hand, and rub his nose. Let him smell you. Not . . ."

She stopped. Gary's footsteps led toward the mule.

"Be careful," Florrie told the boy.

Katie breathed in the cool desert air. Gary offered some soft coos at the mule, and Katie nodded at her sister, and they began the last few yards.

When the body lay in the slight depression Katie had managed to dig, she wiped her hands on her filthy skirt, and strode to Gary and the mule. She took hold of the rope, knelt, and untied it from the wagon tongue.

"I'm tying Bartholomew to the back of the wagon," she told Florrie and her brother. "Just till we're done. I don't want him spooked any more than he already is. You two start getting rocks."

"Shouldn't we cover Ma some more?" Florrie asked.

Katie paused. The two other quilts and the bedroll would smell like death.

"Yes," she said. "By all means. Get the stuff out of the wagon and cover . . ." She stopped. "Hurry. I'll keep Bartholomew here until you're done. Then start with the rocks."

The quilts, bedroll, and blanket served as a shroud. Katie thought about putting the bedroll down first, but that would have meant lifting Ma's body up and out of the pathetic grave. Besides, Gary surmised that all that cloth would keep the dirt and sand and rocks out of Ma's eyes. So they began getting rocks.

That took longer and proved harder than Katie had figured. At a glance, she thought rocks were everywhere, within easy reach, and figured they could have this done in a matter of hours.

Hours had passed, and they had barely got a small wall around the grave.

Then, Gary came racing around the wagon, and tripped over the tongue. He sprang up, screaming, and Katie dropped the rocks she had gathered and rushed toward him.

"What is it?" she cried, and let the boy leap into her arms.

Florrie came running out of the darkness.

"S-s-snake!" Gary stammered.

Snake. Katie sighed. She cursed her stupidity.

"It didn't bite you, did it?" Florrie asked.

The boy's head shook.

"Where was it?" Katie asked.

"I didn't see it. I just heard it. It sounded like a million rattles." Katie patted Gary's head. "It scared me."

"You scared it," Katie said softly. "That's why it rattled."

"We shouldn't do this in the dark," Florrie said. "There are likely more rattlesnakes out there."

Katie nodded. For the big sister, the one in charge, she made some pretty stupid suggestions.

"Let's go to bed," she suggested, and then said

to Gary: "Can I let you down now? Are you still afraid?"

"I'm not afraid," Gary said. "Just wanted to warn y'all."

"Thank you," Katie said.

"Yes," Florrie agreed. "You saved us all."

Katie smiled. Her sister sounded almost like a human being again.

"What about Ma?" Gary asked.

Katie lowered her brother to the ground and looked at the grave.

"She'll be all right." *Florrie doesn't want to move Ma's body back into the wagon,* Katie thought. *Well, I don't blame her for that.*

"I don't want that mean snake to eat Ma," Gary said.

"He won't," Katie said. "Ma's covered with blankets. Florrie's right. Let's go to bed. We'll get up early, and finish Ma's grave."

And after that . . . ?

She shivered.

Grabbing Gary's little hand, Katie led her brother to the back of the wagon. The boy pulled away. The mule looked up sleepily.

"I ain't sleeping back there!" Gary said. "Ma . . . died there."

"Sleep on the ground then." Florrie lost that sound of humanity. "Maybe that snake won't eat you."

"Florrie," Katie said sternly, but she smiled

down at her brother. "Would you like to sleep on the driver's bench?"

"Would I!" Gary grinned.

"Go ahead and climb up. I'll hand you a pillow and some blankets, after I tie up Bartholomew to the wagon tongue again."

CHAPTER EIGHT

They were hanging him.

*Sam MacKinnon kept screaming, begging for mercy. Already he had wet his pants. They just laughed at him, and tightened the noose, which wasn't a noose but a trace chain. The metal bit into his neck. Dropping to his knees, a snot-nosed kid held the Remington .44 in his face. The carved initials—**SM**—had been painted gold and sparkled like diamonds.*

"Ain't this yourn?" the boy said. He laughed, and jumped back to his feet as the men dragged MacKinnon away. "It's mine now!" the boy shouted.

Someone pulled off his boots.

A woman spit in his face.

His mother said: "I told his pa that that chil' of his was no good. Born to hang. Born to hang."

He couldn't breathe. He bit his tongue. The chain cut into his throat. They didn't know how to hang a man. This wasn't the way. The crowd, the noise, the torches, the blood—it proved too much for the horse, which started loping, dragging Sam MacKinnon behind it, picking up speed.

"Stop!" someone called to the horse.

The chain had cut deep, severed his vocal cords. He was choking on his own blood, trying to pray, but managing only rasps. The horse galloped now. MacKinnon rolled onto his stomach. He saw the boulder because night had turned into daylight. He tried to scream, but only tasted blood. The horse leaped over the boulder. MacKinnon's head slammed into the hard granite.

He jerked awake, and almost fell out of the saddle. Would have, had he not instinctively reached out and grabbed the horn with both hands.

"You idiot," he said. He sucked in a deep breath, bent over as his chest felt as though it was cut in half. When he could breathe again, he stared into the darkness.

Honey had stopped. The moon was starting to rise, and it would be a full moon, or near full, anyway. He found the straps and brought up the canteen. After a few swallows, he wiped his face, and wondered how long he had been asleep.

It wouldn't be the first time he had slept in his saddle, but this nap could have killed him. He should have used his bandanna to tie his hands to the horn, to make sure he didn't fall off the mare.

"You keep making mistakes like that . . ." He was rubbing his throat, and couldn't figure out why. He recalled the dream, or tried to, but only remembered a few bits and pieces. None of it made sense. There had been a trace chain around his throat. His mother's voice. He looked at the moon, and almost dropped the canteen.

The moon faced him, low. He saw no trees blocking his view, no boulders, and he could make out the sky.

They were out of the hills, off the mountain.

After lowering the canteen and double-wrapping the canvas, he found the reins on Honey's neck. The horse woke up, and took a few steps without any encouragement from MacKinnon. The hoofs clopped on hard ground.

MacKinnon twisted in the saddle, turning slowly so not to tear up his insides, torment the ribs. He saw the hills off to the south. No glimmers from any candle, lantern, or campfire. He wet his lips and looked to the west, then to the north. He kicked Honey's side slightly, and they started walking.

Clop.

Clop.

Clop.

If he guessed right, San Patricio lay behind him. Bonito City up to the north and west.

And Nelson Bookbinder?

Jace Martin wouldn't risk traveling on a road. He'd cut across the desert. Crooked Cañon. Squaw Cañon. Martin had planned to let the posse think the robbers would be heading to Mexico, but they would turn east. Light out for Roswell. Martin knew a woman in Roswell, and wanted to give her a present before loping off for Texas.

What the hell were you thinking, hitching your life with that team? MacKinnon cursed his stupidity, flicked the reins, and kicked the mare's side. His ribs hurt. They never stopped hurting.

Nelson Bookbinder had Nikita with him, though. Unless Jace Martin abandoned his plan and struck for the Roswell Road, the lawman and the Mescalero would stay south. At least until they got close to Roswell. He remembered hearing someone in Lincoln brag about Nikita. "That 'Pache could follow a fart twenty miles in a blue norther."

Charley The Trey? Maybe Bookbinder led the only posse. Maybe Bookbinder had warned the gambler to leave those outlaws to the law, to Bookbinder himself. Maybe Charley The Trey decided to stay in Bonito City and win his money back.

MacKinnon massaged his ribs.

But if I meet somebody? Posse. Anybody. They don't know me. I'm Sherm Cooper. Was working for an outfit over in the Plains of San Agustin. Decided to light out for the Davis Mountains for the summer. Pretty country down there. Yeah, got tossed from my horse a while back. Ribs damaged. Not the first time. Not the last. Comes with the job. Nah, I'll be all right. Not much a doc can do for busted ribs nohow. Robbery? You

83

don't say. Where? Bo-ni-to City? Hmmm. Never laid eyes on that burg. No, I really haven't seen nobody much. Nobody lighting shuck, nohow. Nah, I don't have a short gun. Pat the rifle. Remember. Pat the rifle. Long gun's more my style. Coyotes. Critters like that. And I remember Haas Engle. We called him Hoss. He had a .44 Remington. No. Not a Remington. Not a .44. Don't even mention a Remington pistol. A Colt. By grab, just make it a Dragoon. Hoss had a big Dragoon, and he was pulling it out of his holster and damned if he didn't blow off his right foot. Yep. They will do that, won't they? Anyway, that cured me of ever wanting to own no short gun. Nice seeing you gents. Good luck catching those thieves.

Honey covered another hundred yards.

"So," MacKinnon asked himself, "why are you traveling at night?"

He studied on that. *I'm no night rider, boys, but have you tried crossing that stretch of land in the summer? Moon's full. And, well, you boys probably never met Betty Bradley in Fort Davis, I reckon. She's worth riding all night for. And this here moon. Almost like daylight with a moon like that.*

MacKinnon softly laughed. He remembered Petey Milligan on that spread up by Tascosa, Petey saying: "Can you teach me to lie like you do, Sam?" And MacKinnon shaking his head,

84

saying: "Can't be taught, Petey. You got to be born a liar. And Ma always said I was a born . . ."

He frowned. He thought of that nightmare. When was the last time he had been wakened by a bad dream?

The moon grew larger. It bathed the road and the desert with pale light. His eyelids kept getting heavier. He said: "You've gone through the possibilities *if* you ain't recognized. What if you are?"

The born liar in him made him smile.

Well, howdy, boys. Been a while. Robbery? You don't say? Where? You mean somebody had the gall to rob Charley The Trey's place. My word. And Billy the Kid's been dead now for how many years?

No. Let's see, last time I ventured into Bonito City was with Budd Bond. You boys remember Budd, don't you? Ornery cuss with the white hair. So me and Budd, well, we . . . yeah, I guess you boys have heard that story more than I've told it. But that was the last time I hit Bonito City. It grown any?

Well, no, I don't recollect seeing anybody. I was working for Skin-Tight Overholser. Yeah, he ain't any less stingy and he works a man like there's thirty-seven-and-a-half hours in a day. Anyway, he had to turn some boys loose on account he said his bookkeeper said he would lose money, and I volunteered. Figured he'd let me finish the month, but, no, that ain't Overholser's style. Cost him seven more dollars, but I didn't mind. Thought I'd see some more country.

Now, that's a darn fool question, don't you think? I know it's night, but I also know a full moon's brighter than the sun this time of year . . . and it sure ain't as hot as that sun. 'Course, I don't get spooked riding at dark. Do you? Ha. Honey has better eyesight that I do, and it's not like I'm putting her into a high lope to see how good she can spy prairie dog holes. I'll keep her going at this pace till past daybreak, find some shade if I can. Rattlers will be cooling off in the scrub just like me. Laze around till the sun starts dipping, and just do 'er all over again.

That's why I enjoy being Sam MacKinnon, boys. I don't have no plan. Thought I could see if they're hiring at the Jinglebob up around Roswell. Maybe head back down to Seven Rivers. And it's been a good long while since I've seen Texas. El Paso. Fort Davis. Or up Tascosa way. Just depends on which way I point Honey.

That's right. You boys laugh, but this mare's stronger than most geldings I've rode. She has an easy lope, a trot that's kind on my arse, and she rarely gives me any fits. I say rarely. You boys see this cut on my eye. I was cutting off a chaw of tobacco and she decided to show me who's queen of the hill. I was. . . .

Boys, you ain't gonna let me finish a story, are you?

Oh, yeah. The old gun and rig? Well, after I left Overholser, I thought I'd try my luck at cards. Over in Tularosa. Yeah, one of these days maybe I'll learn that lesson that you don't play poker in Tularosa. Should've tried to buck the tiger instead, but Milt Yont was running the faro layout and I know he cheats. Anyway, I had a king-high flush. Only one other person had something that looked like a hand. Flush, too, and only one card out there that could beat me. Well, he had it. Now he has my old pistol and my rig. Let that be a lesson to you, gents, and . . . What's that? No. No, I didn't catch the fellow's name. Not even sure if he gave me one, and if he did, it might not have been one he's using now.

What? Oh, well, boys, I had spent some of that money Overholser gave me . . . well, Skin-Tight don't give nobody nothing. I earned those dollars . . . but you know the kind of whiskey they serve in Tularosa. All right, boys, all right. What's your hurry? Oh, yeah, that robbery. Well, he was about my height, but he was missing the tip of his left pinky. I noticed that. Couldn't tell you much anything else about him, though. He didn't say much. Didn't have to. He let that ace-high flush do all the talking for him.

All right, fellas. Good luck. Good hunting. I'll see y'all next time I get the urge to ride back this way.

• • •

He did not try to plan a lie for the chance that some men actually accused him of helping rob The Three of Spades Saloon. MacKinnon would call that bad luck.

He chuckled at his ability. He told Honey: "Can't be taught . . . lying, that is. You got to be born a liar. That's what Ma always said. I was a born liar."

The frown returned.

MacKinnon whispered: "You were born to hang, son. Born to hang."

CHAPTER NINE

She dreamed of sailing across the Pacific Ocean, bound for the Sandwich Islands, so calm, so peaceful, nothing to see but water. She felt at peace, alone on a ship that reminded her of the pictures she had seen in magazines of the *U.S.S. Constitution*, or *Old Ironsides*. The peace did not last. The dream turned into a nightmare as storm clouds blocked the sun, the waves began rocking, slamming against the boat, splashing over the decks, washing her brother, her sister, her mother, her father—her real father, who she barely remembered—over the sides and into the frothing, angry water. She wanted to dive in after them, try to save them from drowning, even though that would be fruitless. She did not, could not, release her grip from the mast. Salt water pelted her, blinded her. She screamed. She screamed. She screamed.

She woke.

Katie rolled against the side of the wagon, hitting it hard. *I'm still dreaming,* she thought, for all around her came the noise of bedlam. She tried to sit up, but felt herself jerked down onto the hard floor of the wagon.

"What's happening?" Florrie screamed.

"Ma!" That was Gary's voice, from the driver's box. "Ma! Ma! Ma!"

The wagon lurched. Monsters howled. Gary kept screaming for his dead mother to help him.

"Katie!" Florrie yelled in the darkness.

"Ma! Ma!"

"Oh." Katie whispered as she tried to push herself off the floor, only to be jerked down again.

"My God."

This was no dream, no nightmare. She came to her knees, groping, hearing Bartholomew's brays, and the snarling all around the wagon. She reached the opening in the canvas cover. The moon lighted up the desert landscape. The mule pulled hard at the rope that tethered him to the wagon, but, by the grace of God, the rope still held. Bartholomew pulled against the rope, jerking the wagon, then kicked his back hoofs at the dogs all around him.

Not dogs.

Wolves.

Maybe coyotes.

Katie wasn't sure. And it did not matter. In the front of the wagon, Gary wailed. All around the aged Studebaker came growls, snaps, barks, and yips. The wolves, or whatever they were, were not just after the old mule, whose hoofs connected against the ribs of one of the wild animals and sent it sailing into the cactus and

90

rocks, where it regained its feet and howled as it limped away. That did not dissuade the others from coming at Bartholomew.

Katie leaped out of the back, fell to her knees, and saw the glowing eyes of a wolf—too big to be a coyote—as it lunged toward her, stopped, snapped, and leaped away. Bartholomew kicked and brayed. From the wagon, Gary screamed and Florrie shouted something unintelligible. Katie found a rock, hurled it at the wild pack. She yelled: "Gary! Stay where you are. Florrie, I need you out here. Now! Grab Bartholomew's rope. Don't let him break free!"

There were more wolves behind Katie, and those were the ones that scared her the most.

She came to her feet, tripped, righted herself and ran toward the glowing embers of the fire. Beyond that, she saw the wolves tugging, snarling, clawing at the quilts and blankets draped over her mother in that shallow grave.

Imbecile. Idiot. Fool. Stupid, stupid, stupid!

Katie stumbled toward the savage animals. Screaming: "Get away! Get away from her!"— as if those wolves cared one whit about her, or could understand her words. Katie staggered and weaved. She dropped to her knees by the smoldering campfire.

How careless, how stupid. She felt worthless. She should have built up the fire, let it burn most of the night, but fuel had become harder and

91

harder to find. That was bad enough, but how could she have left her dead mother covered in blankets on the ground? What had she been thinking? She was nineteen years old—leader of the family now, even if not by choice. She had lived in the territory long enough to know about wolves, about coyotes, about turkey buzzards, ravens and other carrion.

A quick glance at the embers told her she had no time to try to get a stick burning, something that she could wave around and frighten off the animals. She bit her bottom lip, cried out something, and saw the plate.

Instantly she grabbed it, and dug it into the ash and coals like a shovel. Some red and some orange showed, and she felt the heat as she brought the plate up and sent the embers and ash sailing toward the hungry animals and her mother's corpse.

"Leave her alone!" she yelled, and saw flashes of embers and sparks sail through the night and bounce off the desert earth.

She dug into the campfire again. More ash and embers flew toward the wolves—she thought she counted five, maybe six—that leaped away, snarling, growling, as more sparks showered over her mother's shroud. Some of the orange dots landed on the fabric. Katie didn't care. She scooped up more ash, bits of wood, coals, dirt, and grime. This time, the tips of her finger burned from the heat. She did not care about the pain, either. She charged the wolves, waiting until just a few yards separated her from the animals. The coals flew higher, harder, this time, and she flung the plate at the nearest wolf. That animal leaped back, and the plate clattered against the ground and wobbled away a few feet before settling in the dust.

The animals scattered, but did not run far. They slunk about, snarling. Drool seeped from their snouts. Their eyes seemed to glow.

Glancing at the grave, Katie made sure the embers that had settled onto the wool coverings had gone out. She sucked in a deep breath, exhaled, and fought to keep the bile down in her throat.

"You'll have to go through me to get to my mother," she said.

Kneeling, she found the handle of the pickaxe and rose, hefting the heavy tool.

"Get!" she barked. The animals did not back away far. "Scat!"

One growled.

Bartholomew kept pitching, kicking, braying. The wolves near the mule snarled and yelped. She could hear their paws and claws on the hard ground. The wagon creaked and lurched, and Gary kept yelling. Katie did not hear Florrie. She wanted to look back, but could not take her eyes off the wild beasts in front of her.

"Go away!" she yelled, and lunged at the nearest wolf with the pickaxe. It darted away, but another charged forward, barking, its yellow fangs resembling the teeth of a lumberyard's saw. She staggered back, tripped, fell, and the handle of the tool slammed against her left shinbone. Fighting back the pain, she tried to find her feet, but could only get as far as her knees. She managed to raise the pickaxe.

Dust and fear blurred her vision. The air choked her. The noise all around her deafened her. She brought the pickaxe over her shoulder, and swung it down, nowhere close to the lead wolf. The blade struck the rock, causing the handle to vibrate harshly, and she dropped the pickaxe, shook her hands, then again brought the tool up as high as she could lift it—which barely came to her waist now. Furiously, she threw the pickaxe toward the gang of animals. It was too heavy, she realized, and her strength kept fading. The blade landed flatly, and the tool slid a few feet in the dust. The wolves barely moved. Katie, however, lunged back toward the grave and found the shovel. It came up, easily, over her head, and some voice she could not recognize, more beastly than the growls of the wolves, rang across the desert as she charged, swinging the shovel one way and the other.

This time, the wolves shifted back several

yards. She stopped, telling herself not to get too far away. A new sound reached her ears.

"Katie! Katie! Help . . . me . . . !"

Whirling, she hurried back around the side of the wagon. Florrie was on her knees, holding the rope that held the mule. A half dozen or so wolves danced around Bartholomew and Florrie, snarling, yapping, barking. Katie realized that the old mule had pulled away from the wagon, that Florrie gripped the rope with desperate determination. The mule backed away, kicked out at the wolves, dragging Florrie on her knees.

A wolf lunged, came underneath the mule's body between the front and back feet. Its head lifted upward and it snapped at Bartholomew's belly, but the mule leaped up. Florrie lost her grip on the rope, and she fell to the dirt. The mule turned, kicked, turned, and kicked again. By that moment, Katie was sprinting across the ground. Bartholomew swung around, brayed, and Katie dived, both hands reaching out for the frayed rope. Her right hand caught it, and her fingers sprang tight like a vise. By that time, however, Bartholomew had started to turn to flee into the night, to run as far as he could, to Lincoln or Tularosa or all the way to Silver City. Katie felt her dress rip and stones and cactus cut into her stomach as the mule dragged her.

Somehow, she managed to lift her head, and through the dust and pain she saw a wolf leap onto the mule's head. Its teeth must have latched onto Bartholomew's ear, for the mule stopped running and began swinging his head up and down, left and right, but the wolf refused to release its hold.

Katie pushed herself to her knees, pulled the rope, until she braced it against her back, holding it with both hands. The hemp burned through her ruined dress, and carved across her camisole, biting into her skin. She cursed. Blinked. Realized that it was not a wolf holding the mule's ear.

"Florrie!" Katie called out, but barely heard her own voice.

Her sister had managed to grab hold of the headstall. Bartholomew kept trying to shake off Florrie, tossing her like a ragdoll, but Florrie refused to release her hold. The wolves started again.

Katie told herself to let go of the rope, let Bartholomew run. He might escape the wolves. But what would happen to Florrie? Maybe her hands were caught in the leather. Maybe she couldn't let go.

"God!" she yelled.

A cannon roared behind her.

One wolf somersaulted and came up clawing and kicking, in pain, before it scampered away. The noise echoed and rang in Katie's ears. The mule struggled harder. Florrie kept bouncing up and down, but the other wolves quickly backed away. The cannon detonated again, and this time all the wolves—even those behind her and near the grave—yelped and retreated. Pellets bounced off the earth.

Katie moved forward, still clutching the rope. The mule tried to pull this way and that, but Katie and Florrie did not let go. Eventually, realizing the wolves had fled, Bartholomew, exhausted from the fight, stopped kicking and twisting. Florrie dropped to her knees, rolled over, and sobbed. Katie looked at the wagon, and saw Gary leaning against the wagon's tailgate. The double-barreled shotgun lay by his feet.

Trying to catch her breath, trying to shake clarity back into her head, Katie moved toward Bartholomew, and gently reached up and rubbed his neck. "It's all right. You did good," she said, uncertain if she were trying to reassure the mule, her siblings, or herself.

"It's . . . all . . ."

Her knees gave out, and she sank into the sand. She dropped the rope. If the mule wanted to run away now, she could not stop him. She crawled to her sister, and hugged her tightly. A moment later, Gary had joined them, and they clutched each other for support.

"It's my . . . fault . . . ," Katie whispered. "I'm . . . sorry."

"No," Florrie said.

"No," Gary struggled.

Clutching each other, they settled into a cocoon, and somehow, some time later, they fell asleep in the dirt.

CHAPTER TEN

"No coffee?"

Nelson Bookbinder threaded the latigo through the cinch and D-rings without looking at or answering the posse member named Mort. He focused on the saddle.

The one called Davis said: "It got cold last night."

Ignoring those two, Sheriff Nelson Bookbinder waited until he had the saddle snug, then laced the end of the latigo through the keeper, and unhooked the left stirrup from the horn and let it fall against his horse's side.

He stared over the saddle at the two worthless members of his posse. "Ever been to Wyoming?" he asked.

Mort and Davis shook their heads.

"Then you don't know what cold is."

He grabbed the reins to his dun and led the gelding toward the camp. There was no coffee, no breakfast, no fire. Such was the policy of Nelson Bookbinder when he was chasing a felon or felons. He explained, though he did not like to waste his breath on picayune matters. "A hunted man can see a campfire in the night. He can see smoke in the daylight. If he's close enough, he can smell bacon frying or coffee boiling. You ride with me, your breakfast is cold, and you drink water from your canteen . . . if you're lucky enough to have water. When we reached the mountains yesterday, you boys could've turned back to Bonito City with Charley The Trey and the other boys. They didn't like the idea of following those boys into the hills, or leaving all the comforts . . . and profits . . . of Bonito City. But you stuck with me."

Mort started: "Charley promised us . . ." He didn't finish.

"Chew tobacco," Bookbinder said. "Curbs your appetite." He pulled out the plug from his pocket. "Gives your mouth something to do that don't involve idle chatter."

Davis and Mort stared at their boots, as Bookbinder tore off a mouthful of tobacco before shoving the plug back into his vest pocket.

"You want to explain again what happened to that robber you shot?" the lawman asked.

Mort and Davis exchanged glances, then studied their boots before Mort finally lifted his eyes at the lawman and wet his lips. His mouth opened, but that was as far as he got. He grinned and shrugged, as Davis said: "We told you all that when we caught up with you yesterday."

"Yeah." Bookbinder did not blink. "But I'm getting long in the tooth so my memory ain't as good as it used to be. Refresh my memory."

It was not a request. The two oafs looked at

each other. Davis tilted his head at Mort. Mort glared back. Davis shrugged. Mort swallowed and fidgeted with his bedroll as he tried to secure it behind the cantle of his saddle. "Well, it's like we said yesterday. We killed him."

"One shot," Davis added.

"Yeah," said Mort. "One shot. Davis done it."

"Right through his brisket," Davis said.

"And you just left him there?" Bookbinder worked on softening the tobacco with his molars.

"No," Mort sang out. "Not at all. I mean . . . we buried him."

"That's what you said yesterday," Bookbinder said.

"Right," Mort said. "We buried him."

"You caught up with us pretty quickly considering the time it would take to do that," Bookbinder said. "So it wasn't that deep of a grave, I take it."

"Well." Davis took over, as Mort started licking his lips over and over again. "He fell in this hole, you see."

"I see."

"Sinkhole," Mort said, just as Davis cried out: "Fox's den." They glared at one another.

"Something like that anyhow," Davis said. "I thought it was a fox's den, but Mort said it weren't nothin' but a sinkhole."

Bookbinder spit. "You didn't want to bring the body back to Bonito City?" he asked, as he

101

corked the canteen and wrapped the canvas strap around the saddle horn.

"He didn't have no money with him," Davis said.

"Besides, we figured you might need us, too," Mort added.

Bookbinder studied both men briefly. "So you just left him in the . . . this fox den or sinkhole of some kind?"

"We covered him up," Davis said.

"To keep the animals from gettin' him," Mort put in.

"But that hole was mighty deep," Davis said.

"So . . . naturally . . . we didn't fill the whole thing in," Mort said, and his eyes turned murderous as he stared at his pard.

"Think you could find it?" Bookbinder asked.

They studied one another and shrugged. "I don't know," Mort said.

"Maybe," Davis said.

"If no critters don't get him first," Mort said.

For a while, Bookbinder kept chewing the tobacco, and wondering how come a lawman of his stature got saddled with Mort and Davis. Finally, he walked the dun out of their camping spot, and called out to the two worthless liars. "Well, if he didn't have the money, I'm fairly certain that Charley The Trey won't have any interest in his carcass. Come along, gents. We're burning daylight, and it's time to catch up with Nikita."

He waited till the two men mounted their horses and caught up with him. Then he tightened the cinch, and swung into the saddle.

They rode toward the sun, walking at first, then pushing their horses into a trot. Seeing how uncomfortable his two deputies—if one could call Mort and Davis that—looked at posting a trot, Bookbinder kept the dun at that gait longer than he would have otherwise. Eventually, he relented, and reined his horse into a walk.

By then he saw the Mescalero, kneeling beside his pinto gelding about four hundred yards ahead. He studied the country around him, saw nothing that demanded his attention, and put his spurs against the dun's flanks.

He slowed as he neared the Apache, let the dust settle, easing the dun into a walk the last few rods before coming up to the scout.

Nikita did not look up until Bookbinder halted, and the two others caught up a few moments later.

The Apache lifted his right hand and opened his fingers.

Bookbinder nodded. "How old?"

Nikita let the horse apples fall to the ground as he rose, wiping his palms and fingers on his denim trousers. "Last night."

"Just one horse?" Bookbinder asked.

"One bowel movement," the Apache said, which caused Davis and Mort to chuckle like schoolboys before Bookbinder turned his saddle and silenced them with a cold glare.

"Four horses," Nikita said.

"You'd think they'd split up," Mort said.

Bookbinder did not comment.

"Yeah," Davis said. "Send two toward Texas or Mexico to the south, and the other two east."

"Maybe north," Mort said. "Nobody would guess they'd ride north."

"Shut up," Bookbinder said. "Both of you." Bookbinder looked at the horse manure at Nikita's feet, thinking. "You two were right," he finally said to Mort and Davis. "The guy you shot back in the hills, he didn't have the money."

"See," Davis exclaimed in triumph, looking at Mort, "I told you!"

"Maybe," Mort said to the lawman, "you can put in a word to Charley The Trey on account we did dispatch one of 'em vermin."

"It was me that shot him," Davis declared.

"Well, but I seen him first," Mort said, glaring at Davis. "I told you where he was. And I . . ."

"Why don't you two boys ride on ahead a ways." Bookbinder's tone again made it clear that this was not just a suggestion. "Maybe you can dispatch another one of those bad men."

Davis and Mort sank into their saddles, and eyed one another again.

"Boys," Bookbinder said, "I don't see one likely place those thieves could set up an ambush hereabouts. Just ride on ahead. Nikita and I will catch up with you before you're even out of sight."

They rode off at a deliberately slow pace, so Nelson Bookbinder stood, watching and chewing his tobacco. His wife detested the habit, but Bookbinder found satisfaction in its routine. It made him think better. Or more clearly.

"You have good men with you, Bookbinder," the Apache said.

Bookbinder spit juice at the scout's feet.

He had known Nikita since the troubles back in the 1860s, when the Mescaleros had been imprisoned with the Navajos at Bosque Redondo up north at Fort Sumner. Eventually, the Mescaleros got tired of living there and pretty much just left and returned to their homeland. The government, for once, did something right and let the Apaches settle there. After all, the soldier boys at Fort Stanton could keep their eyes on the Indians. When Nelson Bookbinder needed a scout, he got permission from the Army and the agency and he hired Nikita, paying him two dollars a day. The Apache was worth a whole lot more than that.

Nikita could find trails when no one else could. He had more patience than any man Bookbinder had ever known, and Bookbinder, for a lawman, had always considered himself to be an oyster when it came to patience. If a trail went cold, Nikita found a way to warm it up.

If Nelson Bookbinder could make that Apache a deputy sheriff, he would do it gladly—even if he knew it would cost him the election.

"What do you think about the one left in the mountains?" Nikita asked.

"He didn't have the money."

"No." The Apache swung into the saddle. "Do you think those two killed that man?"

"It doesn't matter if they did or if they didn't. He didn't have the money. His pards likely left him behind to slow us down. If Charley The Trey had led this posse, which isn't much of a posse, it would have worked just like those ruffians planned."

Nikita adjusted his black hat. "You white men do funny things to your friends."

"I'm dead certain that's what that fellow they left in the mountains is thinking, too."

They rode slowly. Bookbinder was lucky to have Nikita with him, but luck always played a part in law enforcement. With Nikita's help, he had tracked down a stagecoach robber named Dowdy and had him locked up in White Oaks. They had just stopped in at Bonito City to have Bookbinder's dun re-shoed on their way back to the Mescalero reservation. That's the only reason they had been in the town when the Three of Spades Saloon was robbed.

"Those two." Nikita tipped his head toward the

slow-riding deputies. "Those two will slow us down."

Bookbinder shifted his chaw to the other side of his mouth. "In this country, slow is a good way to go. The horses. Are they being pushed?"

"Harder than they need to be," Nikita said. He looked to the west. "I do not think those two killed that one in the mountains."

"I wouldn't bet against that notion."

"He could have the money," the Apache said.

Bookbinder's head shook, and he removed the pipe, and dropped it back inside his vest pocket. "Those four horses are together," he said. "They didn't split up because one of those horses is carrying all the money."

"If they wanted to go to Mexico, they would start heading south by now," Nikita observed.

Bookbinder's head bobbed. "Which means they're probably riding for Texas."

"Roswell?"

Bookbinder shrugged. "We'll see. That's your job."

"What about the man in the mountains?"

"I'm not wasting my time with him. Seems he already made a bad decision, getting left behind. He'll make another, and it'll cost him aplenty. It's the other four I want, or at least the one with the money."

Nikita looked over his shoulder. "I don't like having a gun behind me."

"You can go track him down if you don't believe he's dead in some hole back there, if you want. Me . . . I don't like having four gunmen riding in front of me, especially when they're heading out of my jurisdiction."

CHAPTER ELEVEN

The sun awakened him. He shook his head, found the canteen, and took a quick swallow.

How many times he had dozed in the saddle during the night, MacKinnon could not count. He recalled being jerked awake by the noise of the sorrel's hoofs on the desert track. That he now found himself still in the saddle and Honey standing in the center of the road, asleep, seemed a miracle. He was tired and he seriously considered turning Honey around and heading back to Bonito City, where he could turn himself in and throw himself at the mercy of Charley The Trey.

MacKinnon yawned. He wanted to wash his face, just a little, but knew better than to waste water. Honey could use a drink, too. The mare snorted, and pawed the earth with her left fore-hoof. Holding the canteen, MacKinnon slowly drew in a breath, and let it out. He didn't shudder. He didn't almost vomit. His bones ached, his left foot was asleep, but he had not felt that sharp pain that made him double over. He wet his lips, and slowly tried to swing his right leg over the back of the sorrel.

That did it.

When he could breathe again, he was leaning

toward Honey's withers, eyes clamped shut, drooling, and desperately clutching the canvas straps of the canteen. Luckily, he realized when his eyes finally opened, he had screwed the cap back onto the canteen. Minutes later, once he could move his left hand away from his ribs, he managed to sit relatively upright in the saddle.

"I'm sorry, girl," he told the horse in a rasping voice. "Maybe we'll find some water up ahead." He knew there were a few water holes along the road, providing they had not dried up. He tried to calculate how far away the closest one might be, but gave up, and wrapped the straps around the horn.

"We'll get you some water soon, girl," he said. "Ribs don't feel as bad as they did yesterday." He shut up. Talking hurt, too. But he told himself that, surely, come evening, he'd be able to climb out of the saddle and back into it. He had busted his ribs before. Once, down around Seven Rivers, he had stoved up his left arm so bad, he couldn't raise it to his shoulder. Yet he had still been able to saddle his gelding and ride at a hard lope. And even with a busted leg, Bad Finger Chaney climbed onto the back of that rank little colt he owned, and rode from Hillsboro to Silver City.

'Course, they had to saw off his leg once he got to Silver City.

He wondered if Bad Finger Chaney was still

hobbling around that burg, sweeping out the stores and stables to earn his keep.

"Let's go, Honey." MacKinnon clucked his tongue, and pressed his spurs against the mare's sides. He kept her at a slow walk, pulled his left foot from the stirrup, and kept twisting in this way and that, and tapping it against the wooden stirrup until he felt the blood flowing again.

Every now and then, he would twist himself as gently as possible and look behind him, to the left and right, and when he saw no dust, no riders, he could breathe a little easier. The sun before him rose higher, forcing MacKinnon to tug down on the brim of his hat. He kept his head bent.

A sun like that could blind a man.

What are the chances that folks in Silver City, or wherever he's hanging his hat, still call him Bad Finger Chaney? Having a bad finger—the pointer on his left hand, think it was his left, was missing the top joint and the rest of that digit was twisted like some juniper branch—ain't nothing when you only got one leg. He ought to be One-legged Chaney. Unless he got himself a wooden leg. Then maybe, Peg-leg Chaney. 'Course, when you think about it, and knowing how Chaney loved to make another fellow laugh, Bad Finger Chaney would be a right fine handle for a man with one leg. Bad Finger? Man's only got one leg, and he calls himself Bad Finger? By thunder, that's a great name.

MacKinnon sighed and shook his head. You came up with all kinds of thoughts, a whole lot of conversations with yourself, when you were hurting all over and waiting for that mountain of trouble to fall atop you.

The sun rose higher. The morning turned hotter.

He wasn't sleeping. At least, he didn't think he was asleep, just daydreaming, maybe resting his eyes. He heard Honey whinny, and jerked his head up when another horse answered.

After blinking several times, MacKinnon saw the rider about a hundred yards ahead. His right hand dropped for the old Remington, and only then did MacKinnon remember that he no longer carried a short gun or holster. He wet his lips, and thought about drawing the Winchester from the scabbard, even though that would hurt like blazes. The rider ahead of him, now maybe fifty yards up the road, stopped.

MacKinnon pulled Honey to a stop.

As far as MacKinnon could tell, the man was alone. He wore a linen duster and a dark hat, probably black, maybe brown. It was hard to tell with the sun behind him. His mount appeared light-skinned, a pretty big horse, too, probably better suited to pull plow or wagon rather than to have a saddle and rider on its back. Honey dropped some horse apples onto the road.

"Hallooo!" called out the rider, who lifted his right hand in a greeting.

MacKinnon sighed. He gathered both reins into his left hand and tried to bring his right hand as high as he could in a friendly greeting. Honey started walking. When MacKinnon knew his hand wasn't going any higher, he lowered it. The rider kicked his big dun into a walk, and the man began singing. It was one of those songs you heard at tent revivals and camp meetings. MacKinnon couldn't recall the name, but a long time had passed since he had attended any camp meeting.

He reined up and tried to think of all the lies he had practiced last night.

The stranger rode ramrod straight in the saddle. He had a long, narrow face, hair the color of gunmetal, with a thick but well-groomed mustache and beard that resembled iron. Underneath the linen duster, he wore black. Black coat, black vest, black ribbon tie, black pants, and black Wellingtons. What MacKinnon could see of the man's shirt was white, or had been. Dusters could keep off only so much dust.

"Howdy," the man said pleasantly, once he stopped singing, and reined up alongside MacKinnon.

MacKinnon tried to return the greeting.

He saw the Bible in the rider's left hand. His right held the reins. He carried no revolver, and MacKinnon didn't see a saddle scabbard. The man's boots held no spurs. And the dun horse didn't look like it could win any races, not even against Honey, as tired as she had to be.

"Who won the fight?" the man asked.

MacKinnon blinked, and shook his head, trying to clear the cobwebs. "Huh?" he managed.

"The fight," the man said. "If you won it, I'd hate to see the other fellow."

MacKinnon rubbed his tongue over his cracked lips. At last he understood, and he cracked a smile, as he brought his left hand up toward the cuts and bruises on his head and face. "Oh," he said. He tilted his head toward Honey's head.

"This mare won the fight."

The man roared with laughter, and stretched out his hand toward MacKinnon. "The name's Yordy, sir. The Reverend Christopher Franklin Yordy."

MacKinnon grimaced, and gingerly brought his right hand around. "Glad to meet you, Reverend," he said, and considered stopping at that. A man didn't ask a stranger's name. If he told you his name, great. If not, so be it. But . . . this gent was a man of the cloth, and MacKinnon didn't need to appear unfriendly. "I'm MacKinnon," he said. A number of names went through his head: Charles . . . Ben . . . Jim . . . John . . . Frank . . . Leach.

Leach? Where did that one come from?

"Sam," he said finally, and was relieved when the reverend gave a gentle shake. "Sam MacKinnon."

"Good Sam MacKinnon," the preacher said, and his head bobbed in approval. "My favorite name. Sam." Holding the Bible high over his head, he began quoting Scripture: " '. . . A certain man went down from Jerusalem to Jericho, and fell among thieves, which stripped him of his raiment, and wounded him, and departed, leaving him half dead.

" 'And by chance there came down a certain priest that way: and when he saw him, he passed by on the other side.

" 'And likewise a Levite, when he was at the place, came and looked on him, and passed by on the other side.

" 'But a certain Samaritan, as he journeyed, came where he was: and when he saw him, he had compassion on him.

" 'And went to him, and bound up his wounds, pouring in oil and wine, and set him on his own beast, and brought him to an inn, and took care of him.

" 'And on the morrow when he departed, he took out two pence, and gave them to the host, and said unto him, Take care of him; and whatsoever thou spendest more, when I come again, I will repay thee."

The Bible came back to the preacher's side. "The book of Luke. Chapter Ten. Verses Twenty-five to Thirty-five."

My word, MacKinnon thought. *You can recite*

all that from memory whilst I can't even recollect
all those lies I thought up last night.

"I named my oldest son Sam," the preacher kept on. "Not Samuel. Just Sam. Thought about naming him Samaritan, but, Rebecca, that's my wife, she did not seem sold on that name, and you're a smart man if you keep your wife happy, so it was Sam. Sam. Sam Ezra Yordy. My kid brother was named Leviticus. And he was a Levite to be sure." His thick beard pointed down the road. "I'm bound for Ruidoso. Bringing the Lord's word to that town. Any idea how far I have to travel, Good Sam MacKinnon?"

Dreading the pain, MacKinnon turned in the saddle, as though looking down the road would give him a better idea of how far it was to Ruidoso. "Ruidoso," he said, and felt a little better when he saw no rising dust, no riders along the road. "I don't think you can make it before sundown, but if you push that horse, it's possible to get there in time to have a hot meal and find a bed for the night."

"Good, good, good. I thank you, Good Sam MacKinnon. I'll have to see what Maccabees thinks and feels." He patted the big dun's neck." He pointed behind him. "I'm coming from Roswell." His head shook. "That's a Sodom if I've ever seen one. Everyone's excited for some baseball game to be played. Baseball . . . a false idol, if you ask me. Gamblers in town. Men

116

drinking in the saloons. I barely got four dollars for all my preaching the Word. I hope Ruidoso is more welcoming to the Word."

MacKinnon tried to think of the right thing to say, couldn't, and nodded firmly as though in complete agreement. He nodded to the east and said: "I'll likely be passing through Roswell myself. Any water in the Río Hondo between here and there?"

The man pondered and thought, thought and pondered, and at length shrugged. "Just here and there, Good Sam MacKinnon, I'm sorry to say. Maccabees drank from my canteen. I'm carrying three. Pays to bring water in this country."

"Yeah." MacKinnon's voice barely carried.

"But I'll give you this warning, Good Sam MacKinnon," the preacher said, and pointed down the road toward the southeast. "Last night, I could not sleep hardly a wink, so I rose, determined to cut that distance to the place where I have been called as much as possible. And I saw the fire of a camp alongside the road. Banditti."

Jace Martin, was all MacKinnon could think, and he felt the anger rising, but he steadied himself, tried to relax, and asked: "What makes you say that, Reverend?"

"Oh, I could see what kind of outfit it was. The moon had yet to set, you see. A miserable excuse of a wagon. Banditti. Banditti, indeed. And the

117

wind carried with it, toward me and Maccabees, the stench of death. Of Hades. Yes, Good Sam MacKinnon, I gave that camp a wide, wide berth, and urged Maccabees into a trot for a good two miles to leave that filth behind me."

Being, MacKinnon thought, *the Good Samaritan that you are.*

"Let's pray, Good Sam, before our journeys carry us in opposite directions."

MacKinnon pushed the hat off his head, felt the latigo tug against his neck, and bowed his head. For as long-winded as the Reverend Yordy could be, at least he kept his praying short and to the point.

Lifting his head, MacKinnon studied the preacher, and before the big man gathered his reins, he decided to take a chance.

"Reverend?"

The man was pulling his big hat low on his head. He turned in the saddle and smiled through his thick mustache and beard.

"I hate to impose on you, sir, but . . ." He massaged his right side. "When Honey . . . that's my mare, here . . . when she won that fight, she must've cracked or busted a couple of ribs."

"For the love of God, son, and you're still riding?"

MacKinnon shrugged. "Well, I've been hurt worse, Reverend. And there's a job waiting for me in Texas, about two days east of Roswell."

Have I ever lied to a sky pilot? Well, yeah, probably.

"Anyway, sir, my horse could use some water and . . ."

"Of course, Good Sam MacKinnon, of course. She can have water from my own hat. You just sit tight and . . ."

MacKinnon held up his hand. "Well, sir, that would be mighty kind of you, but, you see . . . I'd like to step out of this saddle, you see. Check the cinch. And I can water Honey myself from my own hat. And . . . you . . . see . . ."

The Reverend Christopher Franklin Yordy grinned as he dismounted the big dun.

"From one Good Sam to another, Good Sam MacKinnon, I am here to help you. You answer to nature's call, and I shall answer the call of the Good Samaritan and water your mean but pretty as a rose horse. And boost you back into the saddle, if such is your desire."

CHAPTER TWELVE

"Skunk!" Gary Callahan shouted.

Katie poured tea, if anyone could even call this tea, from the kettle into the cups. Her head jerked up and she looked across the emptiness but saw no skunk, no animals, just her baby brother holding his nose.

"Where?" She set the kettle down.

"I don't see it," Gary said, exaggerating the nasal tone of his voice as he pinched his nose harder. "But I sure smell it."

"Stop holding your nose, Gary," Florrie said as she watered Bartholomew. "And grow up."

The stench reached Katie's nostrils now, and she wondered how long the smell had been there, unnoticed. She did not keep her eyes shut for long, because she saw the images of maggots, of flies, and she knocked over the kettle, not caring how much water spilled onto the desert sand, and stepped away from the camp. She wanted to walk. Walk across the land until she came to those white sand dunes between Tularosa and Las Cruces. Maybe the dunes could swallow her up like she never existed.

She stopped, though, after only ten or twenty yards. Florrie and Gary both shouted out her name.

"It's too much," she said to herself. "It's too much. Too much. Too much. Too much."

There were no tears to wipe away. She doubted if she had any tears left, and hardly any water. She couldn't spit. She didn't sweat. All she could do was . . . smell.

"Mama," she whispered, and heard footsteps as Gary and Florrie ran to her.

"Don't leave us." It was Florrie, to Katie's surprise, who spoke. Gary merely grabbed her left hand and squeezed it as hard as he could.

"I'm not leaving you," Katie said. She tried to return Gary's squeeze.

Eventually, she turned around to look at the decrepit wagon . . . the blind mule . . . the over-turned teakettle . . . and the makeshift shroud that covered the putrefying flesh of Margaret Anne Roberts Callahan Truluck, her mother.

She realized she was standing in the road, or what passed for a road in southern New Mexico. Looking east, her eyes traced the little track to the end of the horizon, and then on westward, where she could make out the shimmering of heat, or maybe dust blown by the wind. She knew it was not caused by some traveler, a wagon, a troop of cavalry, a stagecoach . . . anything or anyone who might be able to help.

Hindsight. Had her mother known what was to come, most likely she never would have married

Tommy Truluck. Truluck. Wasn't that name a joke! Then again, maybe she would have gone ahead and married the scoundrel. What was it she had read in one of those silly romance novels she had found in Chloride? You cannot always choose who you fall in love with.

Hindsight. Once Ma had died, they should have left her in the wagon, covered her body, and started walking back west. Florrie had been right. That church, La Iglesia de San Patricio, might have been Catholic, but there would have been people there, people who would understand, who could have helped them. Ma would have been buried by now, perhaps not in the Catholic cemetery, but buried. Not . . . not . . . ripening. That was a word Tommy Truluck would have used.

They could burn the wagon. She had read about a Viking funeral pyre in another romance she had read. That might not be a decent thing to do, but it would mean her mother wasn't going to rot away, or become food for coyotes, wolves, buzzards, or anything like that. Someone might see the flames, come to investigate, find Katie and her siblings and take them back to some kind of shelter.

An orphanage?

She was too old to be in an orphanage. She was practically an old maid already. But could she leave Gary and Florrie at one of those homes?

Even worse, could she let those two watch flames consume their mother's body?

And what if Apaches saw the smoke from the fire? She had heard all sorts of horror stories about those savages. No, no, she told herself, the Apaches were mostly on the reservation. Mostly. Still, she had been in New Mexico when Nana had led his raid across the territory. She wouldn't forget how frightened the miners, and even some soldiers, had been back then. And even if the Apaches posed no threat, what if outlaws saw the smoke from the fire?

Katie let out a weary sigh. A girl could think herself into paralysis.

"Gary," she said, and did the best imitation of a smile that she could manage, "could you go pick up the tea kettle . . . refill it? We'll try again."

"Sure!" he said with gusto. "A full pot?"

"Just enough for three cups," she told him, then tousled his hair and watched him sprint to the wagon.

"That's not a skunk," Florrie said when her brother was out of earshot.

"I know what it is," Katie said.

"We have to get Ma buried. Quickly."

Katie's head bobbed. She wet her lips, or tried to, anyway.

"I'm stupid," Katie said.

Florrie did not disagree.

"The ground has to be softer somewhere than around our camp," Katie said, thinking out loud mainly, but Florrie did not argue. "There's that arroyo over there," the oldest sibling said, and pointed. "Or that might be the riverbed."

"No water if it's the riverbed," Florrie said.

"Not this time of year," Katie agreed.

"But then when the rains come, it might wash Ma . . ." Florrie's head tried to shake away the image.

"If we find softer sand . . ."

"It won't be soft for long," Florrie countered. "We'd hit bedrock before we dig six feet. Maybe three feet. And we can't burn her."

Has Florrie been having the same thoughts?

"What do you suggest, Florrie?" Katie asked.

"That church we passed," she said again. "We put Ma on Bartholomew's back."

Katie was already shaking her head. "Do you think that mule would let us do that, Florrie?"

"He's blind."

"But he hasn't lost his sense of smell," Katie said, shutting her eyes again and massaging her temples as she headed back to the wagon. "And we'd still need water."

"We could make it," Florrie insisted. "You can live a few days without water. We could wait till nightfall. Leave then. We have to do something, Katie. And quickly."

Katie nodded. She crossed the road, and smiled

at Gary as he set the kettle on the hot stone near the fire. "Don't burn yourself," she told him, and moved past the covered body of her mother, behind the wagon, and moved into the desert, between the scrub, the cactus, and the rocks until she came to the edge of the arroyo. The sand was softer here. The question was how deep could she dig until she hit the hard rock. She looked around for stones, too, stones that could cover the body where it was, but what she found, again, were pebbles that would take wheelbarrow loads— and they had no wheelbarrow—before the grave could be covered, or giant slabs of sandstone or boulders that a dozen burly miners or engineers would have trouble moving a few inches. She sighed.

Then she heard Gary shouting, followed by Florrie yelling out for her. Her baby brother was pointing down the road to the west. Katie bolted across the desert. Bartholomew brayed.

"Someone's coming!" Gary shouted as Florrie pointed.

"Who is it?" Florrie whispered urgently when Katie stopped.

Like I'd have any idea, she thought.

She saw the dust, but she could barely make out the rider, who had reined up his horse and appeared to be giving this hard-luck camp a good deal of scrutiny. He wasn't an Apache. At least, Katie didn't think he was.

She ran her tongue over her lips. She had made too many dumb decisions already, and had no plans on doing anything stupid now.

"Florrie," Katie said. "Fetch me that shotgun."

CHAPTER THIRTEEN

Honey stopped at the touch of the reins, and MacKinnon stared down the road at the wagon. Undoubtedly, this had to be the outfit that the Reverend Christopher Franklin Yordy had warned him about, but what might have looked so terrifying to a talkative traveling sky pilot at night, looked downright pathetic to Sam MacKinnon.

A wagon, one front wheel off, with the axle resting on a large boulder to keep the old relic from tipping over. Something of a fire going. A mule. Just one. Two people, who couldn't be more than kids. They were shouting and looking out into the desert somewhere beyond the wagon. MacKinnon couldn't see who they were calling out to, but he figured it was likely the parents. He couldn't hear what they were saying, as the wind blew toward them, carrying away their words.

Then a woman—he could tell by the skirt— came into view. Woman? No, maybe just a girl. Then all three of them were looking toward MacKinnon. He let them look, while he gave the terrain close scrutiny. An arroyo twisted off to the southeast, or maybe that was the bed of the Río Hondo. A person could sit down there, keep a rifle aimed at MacKinnon. Maybe. Or a man with a rifle could be on his belly to the north, hidden by rock or cactus. MacKinnon saw the little boy start for the wagon, but then the kid stopped and turned as the smaller girl headed to the wagon. The boy jumped up and down twice, angry, dragging and kicking his feet as he headed back to the tallest of the three. The girl must have said something, for the boy stepped behind her. The other girl had reached up into the driver's box, and pulled out a long gun.

That's when MacKinnon started to slide the Winchester out of the scabbard. He swore, gritted his teeth, and stopped. Those ribs of his were never going to heal.

The smaller of the two girls handed the long gun to the taller one. MacKinnon left the carbine in the scabbard, and continued to study their campsite. If there had been no fire, no mule, and no people, he would have thought the old wagon had been abandoned. He wet his lips.

"One mule," he said softly, and pondered the situation. The wagon wasn't small enough to be pulled by one mule. Not only that, since the girl—or woman—was holding a long gun, that could only mean that there was no man around here, not in the arroyo, not lying prone and waiting to blow MacKinnon out of the saddle.

Could be, he considered, that someone unharnessed the other mule and rode out for help. But MacKinnon had seen no one on the road, except the parson, and it was closer to San Patricio, Río Bonito, or even Ruidoso than to Roswell.

"You can sit here all day," he said aloud to himself, "or you can be friendly."

Clucking his tongue, he flicked the reins and let Honey carry him closer. When he drew within thirty yards, he reined up again, and raised his right hand as high as he could.

"Halloo!" he called out. "Mind if I come in?"

He could see that the tall girl was maybe just out of her teens, but she was too young to be mother of the little girl and the boy, who kept peeking out from behind her skirt. He could also see now that it was a shotgun, with two barrels, maybe thirty inches long, perhaps even longer. The weapon appeared to be in the same shape as the wagon.

"Come ahead," the tall girl said. She lowered the shotgun slightly, but not all the way, and her fingers remained resting on both triggers.

MacKinnon kicked Honey, but the mare resisted. He spurred her again, and she responded with a snort and shake of her head. He squeezed harder, and she did a quick jump, which blinded MacKinnon temporarily, before she moved on. The mule brayed, but Honey did not answer.

As MacKinnon came closer, he understood why. Something was dead here, and that's when MacKinnon saw the blankets covering what appeared to be a body beyond the campfire.

"Can you help us, mister?" the younger of the girls said. She had red hair, couldn't be older than fifteen. The boy might be three, four, no older than seven. The one with the shotgun . . . well, MacKinnon couldn't rightly tell. All three of them needed a bath.

"Shut up, Florrie," the shotgun-wielder snapped.

Not listening, the redhead said: "Can you help us?"

The little boy stepped between the two girls.

MacKinnon shifted in the saddle. The shotgun started up.

"Ma'am," MacKinnon said, and he pointed at his side, "you can see that I'm not carrying a short gun. My Winchester's in the scabbard. I mean you no harm."

The shotgun stopped its ascent but did not lower any.

"Can you help us?" the redhead said again.

"You traveling alone?" MacKinnon asked.

"No!" the blonde with the shotgun snapped. "Our . . . father . . . he just went back yonder." She motioned with her head toward the arroyo. "To find us breakfast. He'll be back soon. Any time."

"Your mother?" MacKinnon asked.

"She's . . . ," the blonde started to say, but the boy cut her off.

"Ma's dead," the little one said, and his head dropped.

"Gary!" both girls said sharply.

MacKinnon's eyes drifted over again to the blanketed bundle.

"How long y'all been here?" MacKinnon asked.

The blonde considered answering, but held her tongue. The redhead said: "A few days."

MacKinnon looked to the south, beyond the arroyo. He kept the reins in his right hand, and slowly moved his left to cover his ribs. "You haven't seen anybody, have you? Thin man, big mustache, black hat. Be riding pretty hard, most likely, with three other fellows."

They stared at him as though he were mad.

"Or an older guy . . . means business, and an Apache in a black hat? Might have two other fellows riding with him."

The boy's head shook. The redhead said: "Please, mister, we need some help."

MacKinnon looked at the mule, and then his eyes landed on the water barrel. He ran his tongue over his cracked lips.

"Florrie," the blonde said, "keep your trap shut."

"He looks all beat up," the boy said.

MacKinnon smiled as his eyes left the water barrel. "I've felt better." He nodded easily at the sorrel. "Got throwed. There's an old saying among us cowhands, kid. Never been hurt, never been horseback."

"You all right?" the kid asked.

"Gary," the blonde said tightly.

MacKinnon gave a slight nod. "I reckon I'll be fine, boy. But I think I might feel a little better if you could spare some water for me. And my horse."

The redhead jumped up and down. "Please, mister, we're in an awful bad fix here."

"Shut up," said the blonde.

"Katie," the redhead snapped, "we have to have some help. Now."

"Not," the blonde roared back, "from the likes of him!"

"He's got a pretty horse," said the boy.

Honey shook her head, pawed her feet, and snorted.

The younger kids began whispering to the blonde, and MacKinnon sank deeper into the saddle after Honey relaxed. He looked again at the body covered with blankets and some stones. The mother was dead. The father . . . ? Likely not hunting. Maybe not even around. Maybe the mother was a widow.

He should just ride on now, because the blonde certainly didn't want him around. MacKinnon couldn't blame her. She was a pretty good judge of character because she knew that Sam MacKinnon was no . . .

Good Sam.

The thought sent another spasm of pain

through his chest and stomach. He could hear the Reverend Christopher Franklin Yordy reciting his scripture again, talking about that Good Samaritan. Sam MacKinnon shifted in his saddle again.

Well, yeah, black-bearded Parson Yordy gave a mighty fine sermon, but he sure wasn't one to live the way he preached. He could have stopped last night to help this young woman and two kids, but he just rode around them. And the blonde with the shotgun certainly ain't injured like that fellow on the road from Jerusalem to Jericho. No, by grab, she's making it plain that no help is desired from Good Sam MacKinnon.

Besides, what could he do? Busted ribs wouldn't let him work a spade to plant that woman. He wasn't much of a hand at repairing wagons. He couldn't carry the girl and the two kids with him to Roswell or wherever Jace Martin decided to stop.

He was trying to convince himself that someone would be along directly. They'd stop, lend a hand. They'd get these three back down to civilization.

I'm no Good Samaritan, MacKinnon told himself. *I'm an outlaw. I robbed a gambling hall in Bonito City. And I'm out for revenge. The blonde's right. These folks sure don't need any help from the likes of me.*

The three had stopped whispering with each

133

other. MacKinnon looked at the blonde, the red-head, and the boy, and made a gesture at his ribs.

"Look here, I don't mean you no harm, and with these ribs of mine, I can't really offer y'all much help. I can't even climb off my horse . . . not and step back in the saddle again. But here's what I promise to do. Give you my word. I'll send help." He nodded to convince himself. *Yes. That's what I'll do. I can be that much of a Good Samaritan.* "I see anyone traveling west on this road . . . stagecoach, maybe, or some freighters, cowboys, or anyone . . . I'll send them out here to lend a hand." Another nod. He was a born liar, but he could tell the truth. He was telling the truth right now. "My word. And if there ain't nobody on the road, I'll find someone in Roswell. Be there in . . ."

A day would be like a week. For these folks, two days would be like a month. Three days . . .

"You do that," the blonde said as she brought the barrels of the shotgun up a little more, indicating to MacKinnon that he should come closer. Then to the boy: "Gary, fetch his canteen. Fill it from the barrel. Just don't spill any water."

"Katie!" the redhead cried. She was crying. Tears. Real tears.

MacKinnon turned away, and made himself smile as the kid came toward Honey.

"Easy, girl," he whispered when the sorrel caught the scent of the kid. He patted the mare's neck, before he unwrapped the straps and handed the boy the canteen.

"Son?" MacKinnon started to pull off his hat. He got the hat off, but then held it out, apologetically, toward the one with the shotgun. "Umm, ma'am, you think you could spare a hatful of water for Honey here? It's a long ride to Roswell, and I'm not sure the Río Hondo will . . ."

"Florrie," she said, "take his hat, give his horse some water, too."

The girl started as the blonde gestured with the shotgun toward the wagon. "You get close to the wagon, mister," she said. "So we don't waste water carrying over that hat of yours."

He nodded, and made himself smile, though he felt sick in his gut. A tug on the reins and gentle pressure from his legs sent Honey moving, reluctantly, to the wagon. The mule brayed. MacKinnon could hear the gurgling of the water as the boy held the canteen in the barrel. He had had to climb into the back of the wagon, and push his way through the canvas tarp to reach inside the barrel. As low as he was reaching down, MacKinnon figured, there wasn't much water left.

As Gary came up, he held the canteen over the barrel, letting the water drip back in. Then he screwed on the cap, smiled at MacKinnon, and disappeared back inside the wagon. Next, the red-headed girl climbed up the wheel, dunked MacKinnon's sorry old hat in the barrel, and brought it out for Honey, spilling some water onto the sand.

As the horse drank quickly, Gary took the canteen over to MacKinnon. He took one swallow, nodded his appreciation at the boy, and screwed the lid on tightly before securing the canteen to the saddle horn.

When Honey had sucked up all the water, the redhead brought the hat to MacKinnon, who thanked her as he put the hat back on his head. Soaking wet, the hat felt wonderful on his sun-baked head.

Don't think about it, he told himself. *Don't worry about them. You didn't put them in this situation. You dilly-dally here and you'll never catch up with Jace Martin. Thank them, and be on your way. No, you've already thanked them. Just ride. Someone's bound to come along.*

He pulled the hat down tighter, backed the mare away from the wagon, turned Honey around, and nudged her toward the road.

You can't lie yourself out of this one, Good Sam MacKinnon. You're about to become the sorriest excuse of a man. You'll be worse than Jace Martin.

A gust of wind carried sand and smoke past Honey and MacKinnon. It also brought along the smell of the corpse beneath the blankets. That was the last thing Good Sam MacKinnon remembered.

CHAPTER FOURTEEN

The red-colored horse twisted, snorted, and bucked, kicking out its rear legs while lowering its head. The grouchy cowhand, thief, tramp, or whatever he was swore as he lost his seat and rocketed into the sky. By the time he hit the ground with a yelp of pain and rolled over, the horse had bolted down the road.

Florrie screamed, too, and Bartholomew pulled hard on the rope, kicking out at anything that happened to be behind him. Luckily, he was just kicking at air, and Katie swung around the blind mule and gripped the rope with both hands. She saw Gary running toward the road, and called out his name. That was a waste of her breath. The boy couldn't hear her, not with Florrie's shrieks and Bartholomew's grunts and kicks.

The rope burned her hands, and she gritted her teeth, trying to whisper soothing noises to the frightened mule.

Eventually, a tenuous peace settled over the camp, and Katie stroked the mule's neck, and kept her left hand on the animal as she walked past the old creature. She stopped somewhere between the wagon and the road. Her hands found her waist.

Florrie had stopped shouting, but she trembled in her shoes. The man lay on his back, and did not move. Katie moved off, and called out Gary's name. To her surprise, her baby brother stood maybe a hundred yards down the road and another twenty into the desert to the north. The cowhand's horse had stopped running. The boy started toward the animal.

Katie cupped her hands around her mouth, yelling: "Don't you go near that wild mustang!"

"Is . . . he . . . dead?" Florrie choked out.

That broke Katie's concentration. *Is who dead?* She had to think, and shook her head as she yelled: "Gary, you better listen to me!"

Of course, the boy paid no attention. She held her breath as Gary eased closer to the wild horse, which shook its head, pawed the earth, and took a few nervous steps back.

"Gary!" Katie tried again.

The boy kept moving. He must have been saying something to the horse, trying to calm it down. *He'll get himself killed!* Katie thought to herself as she took four fast steps down the road. Then she stopped.

They needed that horse. And her marching like a madwoman after the frightened animal might get Gary seriously wounded, even killed. Holding her breath, Katie watched.

Another gust of wind kicked up. She had to turn her head from the blowing sand, and saw the dust move across the road. The horse stepped back again, and Gary followed. Katie opened her mouth to issue a sterner warning, sucking in air when her brother's hands shot out for the horse.

He had the reins.

"Gary." This time, Katie just whispered his name.

Florrie had managed to move from where she had been standing, and came alongside Katie, who trembled as her brother walked to the horse, and started to rub the wild thing's neck.

"He has the horse?" Florrie said in surprise.

Katie's head bobbed once.

Gary turned around and started back for camp, the reins wrapped around his right hand. When the leather pulled taut, he stopped abruptly and was yanked back.

Katie bit her bottom lip. "Go help him," she told Florrie. "He's too little."

But the boy turned, said something to the horse, and looked back at his sisters. He managed to wave with his left hand, and tried again.

This time, the horse followed.

"How'd he do that?" Florrie asked.

Katie shook her head. "Go," she told her sister. "But don't run. Walk."

"I know how to handle horses, Katie," Florrie said, and headed down the road.

They had a horse now, and they could use that

horse. Florrie wasn't the best rider in the world, but she could do it. She'd have to do it. She could follow the road back to that church in San Patricio. There were a number of small farms in the area. Somebody there had to speak English. They'd send help. They'd . . .

She turned and saw the saddle tramp just lying there.

Dead?

Katie watched him a long time before she saw his chest rising and falling. Yet she still had not taken one step until she heard the *clops* of the red-colored horse and Gary whistling, or at least, trying his best to whistle. She looked away from the intruder and made herself smile at her brother, before turning to Florrie.

"Tie that horse to the other side of the wagon. Not near Bartholomew. I don't know how they'll get along."

"Should I water him?" Florrie asked.

"He just drank some of *our* water," Katie answered, and looked back at the stranger.

"Is he dead?" Florrie asked again.

"No." Katie moved to him, and knelt.

She was leaning away from him, sitting on the ground, rubbing her forehead, when Florrie and Gary came up behind her.

"Did you see how I got that horse, Katie?" Gary asked.

She lowered her hand, nodded, and made

herself say something, although she didn't know exactly how it came out or what she had actually said.

"How is he?" Florrie asked.

Katie shrugged. "He's alive."

"Well, are you going to help him?" Florrie demanded.

"Like he helped us." Katie felt the acid on her tongue. She turned her head and spit into the dust.

"Well . . . ," Florrie said.

Katie twisted her head and looked up at her sister. "Can you ride back to that church?"

"Ride what?"

"His horse!" Katie practically screamed.

"That wild thing?"

"It's not wild," Katie said. "It just got . . ." She smelled the stink now, and tried to think of something else. "It . . . it was that . . . wind. You can ride."

"You can ride, too."

"I have to stay here. And you ride better than anyone in our family. Even Ma said so." She closed her eyes, tried to calm herself and steady her breathing and her voice. "Florrie. It's not that far. You could be there before sundown. I'll stay with Gary . . . with him." She nodded at the stranger. "You just bring back help."

Florrie turned, looked at the horse, and shook her head. When she faced Katie again, she pleaded: "I can't, Katie. Do you see those stirrups? How long they are?"

Looking at the stranger's horse, she stared at the saddle. It was old, probably had been made especially for him. She could see the laces and knew her sister was right, but Katie couldn't hide the desperation in her voice. "Can't you shorten them?"

To Katie's surprise, Florrie walked closer to the wild horse that now seemed contented and maybe even asleep. Katie frowned when Florrie's head shook, and she turned away from her sister to look at the man, who remained unconscious.

"No," Florrie was saying. "Even if we got the leather laces out, they wouldn't come up short enough for my little legs. You might be able to ride her though."

Katie let out a humorless chuckle. "You've seen me ride."

"I bet he had that saddle made for him," Gary said. "Special."

Katie snorted. "Yeah, a hundred years ago." She looked at her sister. "You don't need the stirrups."

"On a horse like that anyone does," Florrie said. "You saw how that horse bucked. And I sure won't try riding that monster bareback."

"All right." Katie made herself look at the man. "It was a stupid idea." She wiped her face.

"Well," Gary said.

"Well what?"

"Are you just going to sit there and watch him all day?"

Florrie added: "And hope he dies?"

Katie swore underneath her breath, and leaned closer to him. Her hand reached out, hesitated, and finally came to his shirt. She could smell his sweat, that rank odor of the unwashed. Her hand moved to his forehead, and she felt the knot on the side of his head, about the size of a pecan. His eyes fluttered, her hand shot back to her side, and she heard him mutter words that made no sense—a name she couldn't quite catch. His head turned one way and the other, and she wondered what would happen if he woke up.

She was about to learn. His eyelids moved, and he stared at the sky briefly before finally turning toward Katie. His mouth opened, but if he was thinking about saying something, he decided to just let out a long, heavy sigh.

"I ain't no Good Samaritan," he said. "You'd be smart to . . ."

He slipped back into that void.

Katie's shoulders sagged. She leaned back, shook her head, and found that resolve again.

"Florrie," she said, "heat up some water in the kettle. Gary, I think we still got some of the salve Ma always liked to rub on us somewhere in that carpetbag. And, Florrie, there's Ma's old camisole. If you can find it . . . I don't have any

143

notion where it might be in that wagon . . . just tear it into strips about this wide." She measured the distance with her hands. "We can use those for bandages."

"He was holding his side," Gary said, and showed her about where on his own tiny body.

"Right," Katie said. "Busted ribs. Maybe we should wrap them up. I don't know." She pursed her lips. "We still have some soap somewhere, too. Put that in a bowl with the hot water."

"You'll have to take off his shirt to wrap his ribs," Florrie said in utter disgust.

"Uhn-huh." Katie nodded. "Get that knife. The one that's sharp."

It wasn't the devil kneeling over him. Of course, it wasn't St. Peter, either. Long minutes passed before the figure came into focus, and he recognized the blonde-headed girl as she placed a cool, wet rag on his forehead and dabbed away the dried blood, the filth, the grime with gentle fingers. She knew he was awake, knew he kept staring at her, but she ignored him as she pulled the rag away and wrung it out, letting the water drip back into a bowl.

He studied her hand. Sunburned. Scratches with the scabs broken. He could make out the rope burn between her thumb and forefinger. The hand returned with the same rag, wet again, and he noticed the blackened thumbnail. She'd probably lose it, but he doubted if she would care one way or the other. As her hand gently swabbed at the wounds on MacKinnon's face, she brushed the bangs from her forehead with her other hand. Still, she did not look at MacKinnon.

He looked the other way, seeing the front wagon wheel and the legs of the mule. The other two children had to be somewhere around, but he saw no trace of them. He smelled the smoke from the fire and heard the faint crackling of burning wood. The sun he could not find, but from the color of the cloudless sky and the length of the shadows, it had to be late afternoon.

His head throbbed unabatingly while his right side tormented him only when he breathed. Every muscle in his legs ached, as did his lower back, and he knew he would not be climbing into a saddle any time soon.

With the rag going back to the bowl, MacKinnon turned his head again. Honey? He couldn't quite piece together everything that had happened. He thought he might have been riding away. The wind had spooked his mare. And . . . and the smell. The stink of death. That's what had caused Honey to buck him off. That had to be what had happened. Why else would he be here on the ground? A twinge in his ribs caused him to grimace, but the dampness and coolness of the water-soaked rag relieved him for a moment.

His eyes found the blonde, but she kept refusing

to acknowledge him. MacKinnon couldn't blame her for that.

His lips parted, he swallowed with difficulty, and he made himself break the silence. "Why are you doing this?" he asked.

It took a while before she answered. MacKinnon wasn't sure she was going to, and when she did, she still refused to make eye contact.

"It's what people do." She returned the rag to the bowl and then squeezed the water out of it.

Not everyone, MacKinnon thought. His ribs throbbed. After flexing the fingers of his left hand, he brought it to his chest. He felt his skin, and knew his dirty old shirt had been removed, as had his filthier muslin undershirt.

The girl spoke. "I don't know if wrapping those ribs is the right thing to do or not. I don't know if they're broken or cracked or just bruised."

He made himself smile. "I'm fairly certain they're more than just bruised."

Smiling would be foreign for her. He couldn't blame her for that, either.

"I had to cut off your shirt," she told him. "Didn't want to pull it off over your head."

At least she was talking, even civilly, to him. He licked his lips. She looked at him now, leaving the cloth in the bowl. She tried to think of something to say, or maybe she was waiting for him to say something. He thought of what he should say.

"Thank you."

Her eyes rolled.

"I take it my horse took off for parts unknown."

Her head tilted. "Gary caught him up. Her up, I mean."

His eyebrows arched, and he looked around, trying to find the sorrel.

"On the other side of the wagon," she said, gesturing with her head.

He couldn't see Honey, but he didn't think the girl would lie to him. He wet his lips again. He could use a drink of water, or, better yet, something more potent, but he couldn't push his luck. He thought about asking her again to explain why she would bother to help him. Instead he asked: "Gary's your . . . ?"

"Brother," she said. "Five years old."

"How . . . ?" His tongue and throat failed him.

Shaking her head and letting out a tired sigh, she turned to retrieve a canteen—his canteen, MacKinnon understood, but the water in it had come from the barrel, the property of the three siblings. He watched in silence as she unscrewed the cap. She shifted over and used her free hand to raise his head while her right hand tilted the canteen. He swallowed once, twice, then his head was being lowered and the canteen pulled away. He closed his eyes, listening to the wind, the cap being screwed tightly, and the crackling of burning wood. There were voices, too—soft, like one might hear in church.

Now he realized the blonde's eyes were burning through him, and he stared back at her. His lips moved, his tongue shrank, and he asked again: "How long have you been here?"

"A few days," she told him.

"Your . . . folks?"

Her head turned north. She did not blink. Nor did she cry. But he could see her lips trembling and the worry scratched into her furrowed forehead.

"Ma died," she said at length. She looked back down at him. "It was her lungs. She'd been sick for a long, long time."

"And your . . . pa?"

Her head shook. "My father's dead. A long, long time. The cad Ma was married to . . . he's gone."

"For help?" MacKinnon asked.

"To hell," she said. "Or so I hope." She reached for the rag, picked it up, wrung it out, and dropped it back into the bowl.

"If you can stand, I'll bring your horse over," she told him. "There's enough light left in the day that you can cover some ground."

His head bobbed. Night riding certainly suited MacKinnon.

"The no-good left behind some clothes. He's skinnier than you, but I think they'll fit good enough." She stood, brought her hand up to shield her eyes, and called out to her little brother.

"Gary, fetch one of your pa's old shirts. Florrie, get his horse. He's riding out."

It didn't sound to MacKinnon as though he had a choice. He tried to push himself up, but his ribs wouldn't let him. He let out a gasp and collapsed back on the blankets underneath his old body.

"What?" she said, staring down at him with more hatred than he had ever seen in a woman's eyes.

"Maybe . . . ," he said. "Maybe . . . in the morning."

CHAPTER FIFTEEN

Four-Eyes Sherman's horse dropped, and even though the old fool should have been expecting this, he barely managed to leap out of the saddle and avoid being rolled over by the dying animal.

Which, Jace Martin thought, might have been better for everyone had that happened.

After reining up, Martin twisted in the saddle. He swore, turned around, and called out to Chico Archuleta, who was riding a few yards ahead. "Hold up!" Looking back at Sherman and the gelding, Martin cursed again.

The youngster, Harry Parker, slid off his gelding, and started back toward Sherman, but stopped when Martin told him: "Don't waste your strength, boy. Not till we make Juarez Spring." Martin pulled off his black hat, and wiped his wet forehead and sticky hair with his dusty shirt sleeve.

Sherman had managed to sit up, and now he dipped his fingers inside his shirt pocket and slowly withdrew his spectacles. The old man's shoulders sagged, and he dropped the eyeglasses between his legs. "Busted," he managed to mouth, and dropped his head.

Martin returned the hat to his head, pulled on the ends of his black mustache, and looked back east. He saw no dust, but a man like Nelson Bookbinder, and especially that Mescalero scout, wouldn't raise any dust. He glanced at the saddlebags in front of the saddle, and looked up the trail at Chico Archuleta.

"How far . . . ?" He had to stop. Those two words had scarred his throat. He reached for the canteen, but stopped himself, stared back at the Mexican, and started to finish his question.

He didn't have to. Chico Archuleta understood. "*¿Quién sabe? Seis o siete* kilometers."

That wasn't too far. Martin started to pull up the canteen, but stopped when he looked back at Four-Eyes Sherman and saw him drawing his revolver.

"Not the gun, you old fool!" he barked, and moved his right hand to the butt of his Schofield. "If that law dog is anywhere near here, he'll hear the shot."

Four-Eyes Sherman stared.

"The knife," Martin told him. "Use your knife."

Parker dropped the reins to his gelding and walked over to the horse. The kid's horse dropped its head. Cakes of foamy sweat covered the gelding's neck. The horse sure wasn't going to wander off, and Martin wondered if Parker's mount could even get the four or five miles to the water hole at Juarez Spring.

Four-Eyes Sherman shifted, and reached into his pants pocket. He struggled but eventually

151

drew out a large pocket knife. It must have taken him two or three minutes to get the blade open. The man squinted as he stared at the horse just a few feet away from him. Sherman's lips, cracked and swollen, trembled, and he looked up at Martin for help, then back to his horse, up at Harry Parker and even over at Chico Archuleta. When he looked back at Martin, he whispered: "Please."

"He doesn't need a knife." Harry Parker looked from Sherman's horse to Martin. "It's dead."

The old man's shoulders sagged, and the knife slipped into the dirt.

Parker moved to Sherman and held out his hand. The kid would need to grow up fast, and figure out that helping a fool like Four-Eyes Sherman wouldn't do him any good in the long run. A man's first priority was his own hide. But Sherman took the kid's proffered hand and let himself be pulled to his feet.

Sherman staggered over to his horse and started to reach for his canteen.

"Pour the whiskey out, Four-Eyes," Jace Martin told him.

Slowly, the old-timer straightened, turned, and did his best to wet those ugly lips with his tongue.

"If you'd put water in that canteen," Martin said, "you might not be afoot. Let's go. We've burned enough daylight. See you at Juarez Spring."

He smiled once he had turned around and kicked the buckskin into a walk. *If you live getting there,* he thought.

Once he reached Chico Archuleta, Martin reined in to look behind him. "Idiot," Martin said, and swore underneath his breath.

"*Ambos son tontos,*" the Mexican said.

Harry Parker, green as a pea, had let Four-Eyes Sherman climb up behind him. The gelding labored, but kept plodding along.

Shaking his head, Jace Martin clucked his tongue and kicked his mount into a walk again. Chico Archuleta rode beside him. Neither said a word. It was too hot, and they were too tired to talk anymore. Neither looked behind them. It was too hot, and they were too tired to move. And the long and the short of things was simple: If Harry Parker and Four-Eyes Sherman did not make it to Juarez Spring alive, there would be more money for Martin and Archuleta.

You could find water in this country. If you knew where to look. Apaches knew where to look, but not Jace Martin. Well, he knew the main places, those he had been told about, those where he had slaked his own thirst, and those on the map he had bought at the trading post in Tularosa. To the north he could find the Río Hondo, and down south, the Río Felix and the Río Peñasco. They flowed, intermittently, at least, but rarely this time of year. But Jace Martin was riding in the wasteland between the Hondo and the Felix. East he knew he would find water in the Pecos and at Roswell, but the river and the town were one long, hot, dry ride from here.

He had planned it this way, though. A man didn't make his pile without some struggles. The way Jace Martin had figured things, Charley The Trey would come after him and his *compadres* as soon as he could catch up horses and enough men with iron and sand. Martin would buy some more time and miles by leaving Sam MacKinnon in the mountains south of the mining town. Charley The Trey might not quit so easily, but most of the men the gambler would have rounded up in Bonito City would turn back once they realized that the thieves were striking out through the desert. And eventually Charley The Trey would figure out he was losing money chasing the thieves when he could be cheating customers at his saloon and getting most of that stolen money back.

But Nelson Bookbinder and his Apache had been in town, too—at least Sam MacKinnon had said they were there. So Bookbinder would be leading that posse.

Trying to swallow, Martin again looked at the saddlebags with the money he had stolen from Charley The Trey. He still had not found time to count it, to see how much richer he was.

Because even the best-laid plans . . .

Or however that saying went.

He wanted to look back, not to learn how much farther Parker and Sherman had fallen behind, but to see if the posse had come into view. Jace Martin wouldn't do that, though. Looking behind you meant you were nervous at best, scared at worst.

Martin let out a rough laugh, which sounded more like a cough, and shook his head. But even Bookbinder would have a hard time keeping his posse together. They might give up and ride back to the shade and coolness of Bonito City. The lawman and the Apache? They wouldn't.

He found his canteen, and drank again. He knew he should dismount and let his horse have a swallow, too, but Martin didn't want to waste time. Juarez Spring would be coming into view pretty soon. The buckskin could drink then.

The spring lay at the end of a box cañon—which really wasn't much of a box or a cañon—in the rough, broken land southwest of Roswell, and on a northwest line from Artesia. The water might have been brackish, but it was wet, and enough for the snakes that lived here. Enough to get a man and his horse real water.

Or had been.

Chico Archuleta reached the spring first, quickly climbed off his horse, and stumbled to the opening in the rocks. Jace Martin felt the urge to spur the buckskin into a lope to cover the remaining twenty yards when he saw the Mexican push himself from the prone position to his knees, lift his head to the cloudless sky, and make the sign of the cross.

"No . . . ," Martin said.

Archuleta's horse showed no interest in the spring. Martin's own mount made little attempt to hurry to the water, and horses can smell water. Martin choked back a curse, but let his buckskin cover the distance so he could see for himself.

Decades earlier, Juarez, whoever he was, had dug out the spring and made something of a cistern with rocks from the cañon. Martin made out the scattered skeleton of a jack rabbit or something, saw the withering shrubs. Even the cactus looked parched. At least, they had some shade in the cañon.

They just didn't have any water.

"Dry," he said, and shook his head.

"*Sí.*" Chico Archuleta rose, and staggered toward his horse.

"Well . . ." Martin nodded. "There's water in Roswell." He looked south. "Artesia?"

"Roswell is . . . closer," Archuleta said. "*Un poco.*"

Martin agreed. "And maybe there's water in the Hondo."

The Mexican stared blankly. "We are too late for the spring runoff. And the summer monsoons?" He looked at the sky and shrugged.

Archuleta knew this country better than Martin did, but both of them knew one thing. Roswell might be closer than Artesia, and the Río Hondo might have some water running up north and east, but the horses they were riding would never live to see Roswell or the river. And whether Martin and the others made it would be even money.

Twisting in the saddle, Martin looked toward the entrance of the cañon. The kid, Parker, had wised up, and he now led his gelding, and Four-Eyes Sherman was holding the bay's tail, letting the horse pull him along. They were about a hundred and fifty feet from the spring.

"I will tell them not to waste . . ."

"Let them come," Martin said, and he grinned at the plan that he had already started to formulate.

"¿*Porqué*?" Archuleta looked up, his eyes wide.

"Just let them come. Let their tracks lead all the way to the water. Then we'll just mount up, revived by the fresh water at Juarez Spring, and ride out of the cañon and keep on toward Roswell, fresh as a daisy."

"Get on behind the kid," Martin told Four-Eyes Sherman.

"Jamie's played out," Harry Parker protested. "He'll never make it to Roswell carrying the both of us."

Hatless, the kid's face was already red and

ugly, while Four-Eyes Sherman looked different without his spectacles.

Martin laughed. "He won't make it carrying you, Parker. But he'll carry both of you out of this cañon."

"I . . . need . . . I need . . . water," Four-Eyes Sherman said.

At least the old man still carried his canteen. Empty of rot-gut liquor, but still capable of holding water.

"We all do," Martin told him. "And I'm feeling generous."

He swung to the desert, removed his canteen from the horn, and held the canteen toward the old-timer.

The sun had burned his face, too, and he took a step back, suspicious.

Martin laughed and shook the canteen, letting the water slosh. "Drink. It ain't poison. I know what I'm doing."

Sherman came closer, started to lift his hand, hesitated until Martin shook the container again. That was all it took. Sherman snatched the canteen, almost dropping it, and stumbled backward, managing somehow to stay upright despite his weakness.

"Two swallows," Martin said when Sherman began to pull out the stopper. "Just two. And not big swallows. My horse gets a drink after you."

To Martin's surprise, Four-Eyes didn't turn

greedy. His Adam's apple bobbed twice, and he smiled, lowered the canteen, pushed the stopper back in, and even thanked Jace Martin.

They rode out in the middle of the cañon. Martin even kicked the buckskin into a lope until he reached the entrance, where he reined up, stood in the stirrups, and looked west.

Once his companions caught up with him, Martin sank back into the saddle, and kicked the horse into a walk. They turned north, worked their way around the cañon, until Martin stopped again. This time, he dismounted, started to unsaddle the horse, saying to the others: "We'll rest here."

No one argued. It was too hot to protest.

Martin waited and listened.

When the sun disappeared, and the desert turned cool, Martin told Sherman, Archuleta, and Parker what he planned to do. The buzzards wouldn't be flying now, and, with Juarez Spring dry, maybe the coyotes and carrion wouldn't be nearby, either.

He pulled a knife from its sheath, and walked to the horses.

Chapter Sixteen

Mort said: "My head is overcooked."

Davis said: "So's mine, and I'm wearin' a black hat."

"That's your own fault," Mort said.

"Well, it ain't my fault that we ain't caught up to 'em robbers yet," Davis said. "And I shot my man. Killed him dead."

"Did not," Mort said.

"Did, too," Davis said.

Mort said: "Well, maybe you did."

Davis said: "Ain't no *maybe* to it, Mort."

Said Mort: "It's too hot to bicker."

Said Davis: "At least your hat ain't black."

Nelson Bookbinder turned in the saddle. He didn't have to say a word. Mort and Davis fell silent and began studying the ground in front of their horses.

They climbed a hill, crested it, and Bookbinder reined in. He took in the scene below in an instant, and stood in the saddle to study the land beyond.

"Criminy," Davis said.

"Is that a dead horse?" Mort asked.

Davis said: "Maybe one of the robbers is under the horse."

Bookbinder did not look at the two posse

members at his left. He kicked his horse into a walk, moved down the easy incline, and pushed him into a lope to cover the three furlongs to where Nikita stood over a dead horse.

"How long?" Bookbinder asked.

The Mescalero pointed at the sky. "No buzzards yet. Two hours."

"By jingo," Mort said, "we're gainin' on 'em, and now they's ridin' double. Let's get a-movin'."

"Go on," Bookbinder said. "You want to be afoot in this country, get a-moving."

The man frowned. Davis grinned, but only until Bookbinder turned to him.

"Juarez Spring?" the lawman asked.

The Apache shrugged. "Maybe so."

Staring off to the east, Nelson Bookbinder saw the afternoon haze, the distant mountains, the heat shimmering. He kicked his horse into a walk. The Apache swung onto his horse, and they rode on. They rode as if they were in no hurry.

The sun had started to sink when they came to the entrance to Juarez Spring. Pointing at the tracks, Nikita said: "Rode in. Rode out."

Bookbinder's head bobbed. "Catch them tomorrow."

"If they're still alive."

"Let's let our horses get their fill. This is probably the last water we'll find till we get closer to Roswell."

When they reached the spring, Bookbinder spit into the wind.

Davis swore.

Mort groaned. Said: "I don't want to die like this."

Davis said: "You reckon 'em swine dynamited the well so we'd die of thirst."

Bookbinder cursed the two posse members for fools, then dismounted. Keeping his left hand on the reins, he stepped closer to the Apache who knelt in front of this ancient cistern old man Juarez had built years and years earlier. Nikita pressed his hand into the sand.

"What do you think?" Bookbinder asked.

The scout nodded. "Fool white men," he said, unsheathed his knife, and sank the blade into the sand. Bookbinder found his own Bowie knife and knelt across from the Mescalero and dug into the ground. After a minute, he looked up at Davis and Mort and said: "If you want water, start digging."

When the night sky began turning gray, Nelson Bookbinder tossed off his blanket, and stretched his stiff muscles. He swore, found his revolver, pulled the hammer to full cock, and rose. After kicking Mort awake, he whispered: "Get your pard up." He moved to the edge of camp.

A moment later, he knelt by Nikita's crumpled body.

• • •

He let the Apache drink the warm, muddy water from his canteen.

"Getting old," Nikita said.

"Uhn-huh," Bookbinder said. "So am I."

"Where's our horses?" Mort called out.

Davis cursed. "You let 'em steal our horses!"

Bookbinder corked the canteen. "Shut up."

The Apache rubbed his head. "I heard them." He flinched when his fingers found the knot on his head.

"You should've woke us all up," Davis said.

The Apache said: "I thought you were up. You had the second shift of guard duty."

"Well . . . I . . . well . . ." Davis looked to Mort for help, but Mort cursed his pard for being a lazy, worthless tramp.

"I don't want to hear one word from either of you," Bookbinder told the two.

Nikita sighed. He had been asleep. One of the horses snorted, so he had drawn his knife and started for the picket line. He had thought it would be easy. But as he moved toward the one trying to put a rope over Bookbinder's horse's head, he only knew blinding pain and then a fitful sleep until Bookbinder began gently slapping his face minutes ago.

"We underestimated them," Bookbinder said. "I underestimated them."

"What are we going to do?" Mort cried out.

Bookbinder spit. "I'm going to fill my canteen. It ain't the best water, but it's wet." He looked down at the scout. "Can you walk?"

Nikita nodded.

"We're gonna die," Davis whined.

"Die if you want," Bookbinder said, "but Nikita and I are walking out of here."

They soaked their bandannas in the spring and retied the cloth around their necks. After they had swallowed a few mouthfuls of water and refilled their canteens, they started to walk out of the box cañon.

Bookbinder stopped and looked at Mort and Davis in the graying light. "You plan on carrying your saddle and tack?" he asked. "All the way to Roswell?"

Davis stared at Mort.

"Store it in the rocks," Bookbinder said, and pointed. "You can come back for your gear later. It might even still be here. I'd lose your spurs, too."

The two men did as they were told, and began walking toward Bookbinder and the Mescalero. The lawman shook his head.

"Maybe you're forgetting something?" he said.

Mort and Davis looked at each other and then back at Bookbinder.

"Your long guns?" Bookbinder said. "There's a chance you might have need of them. I doubt it. But there's a chance."

They had water, which the robbers and now horse thieves had not counted on. When Bookbinder saw buzzards circling he forgot all about Mort and Davis.

"Interesting," Bookbinder said.

The Apache nodded. "Like you said, we underestimated them."

"At least one of them," Bookbinder said.

Mort fired his pistol in the air, and the turkey buzzards flapped their large, ugly wings and flew away.

Nikita delicately moved around the bloated carcasses of the horses, looked at Bookbinder, and drew his pointer finger across his throat.

"Smart," Bookbinder said.

The Apache nodded.

"What . . . ?" Davis looked to Mort for help. "You mean . . . they cut the throats of their own horses?"

"Smart," Bookbinder said again.

"Smart?" Mort said. "That's downright criminal."

"Maybe," Bookbinder said. "But they knew we'd be coming." He glanced at the Apache. "What do you think? Dusk?"

"Around then," the Mescalero answered.

"He slit the throats," Bookbinder said. "Didn't want them to whinny and let us know they were still in the area. Waited till dark, snuck into our camp, made off with our horses, put their own saddles on, rode away. Smart."

"Not too smart," Nikita said. "They didn't realize that Juarez Spring wasn't completely dry."

Davis thought about this. "So they . . . they still don't have no water?"

"Some," Bookbinder said. "But not much."

"Well . . . ," Mort said. "What do we do now?"

Nikita drew his knife and moved to the buckskin.

"We'll stay here," Bookbinder said. "No sense in moving afoot now. Sun's already hotter than the hinges of Hades. We'll eat some horsemeat, stay in the shade, start walking when it cools off."

"We'll never catch 'em," Mort said, and pointed at Davis. "And it's all your fault."

"Somebody'll catch them," Bookbinder said.

"I don't want to eat no horse meat," Mort said.

"You don't have to," Bookbinder said.

CHAPTER SEVENTEEN

He woke with the dawn, and, keeping his elbow on the ground, lifted his right hand toward the closest spoke in the front wheel. His lips tightened, as he found that he could push his arm up and grip the next spoke. And the next. He knew one more spoke was as much as his ribs would allow. His lips flattened, his eyes closed, and he pulled.

A couple of blasphemies and one horrible yell later, he was sitting up. The world spun, but he didn't fall onto his back. He didn't throw up his supper, either.

Did I have supper? he thought. He couldn't remember.

Footsteps made his head turn, and the little boy slid to a stop a few feet from him. The kid's mouth hung open, and his eyes looked like saucers for teacups.

" 'Morning." MacKinnon smiled. He did not dare laugh. "I wake you?"

The boy's head shook. "But you scared me."

"Scared myself," he said, and held out his right hand. His left he hugged tightly against the bandaged ribs. "You reckon you could help me to my feet?"

The boy looked behind him.

"Go ahead," came a voice. "He ought to be going before the sun gets too high." That would be the blonde. He didn't see the redhead.

"Your name's Gary, ain't that right?" MacKinnon asked, as the five-year-old took a few tentative steps toward him.

"Uhn-huh. Gary. Gary Truluck. My sisters are Callahans. On account we got different pas."

The small hand took hold of MacKinnon's and squeezed as hard as a boy that age could manage.

"All right, Gary," MacKinnon said. "My name's Sam. But you can just call me MacKinnon. Back up, if you would, Gary, and start a-pulling."

He cut loose with three more oaths, but when Gary let go, Sam MacKinnon was on both knees, and he kept up with the profanity until he found himself standing. He swayed, but spread his feet apart, wondering if all miracles hurt this much.

"My ma would make you wash your mouth out with soap," Gary told him, and MacKinnon nodded.

"So would mine."

He looked at the boy, but Gary's head was bowed, and MacKinnon knew the kid was trying to stop the sobbing. His left hand reached over and he touched the kid's shoulder, squeezed it softly, and then tousled the boy's hair.

"You got a hat, Gary?"

The head bobbed but did not look up. Gary's tiny hand reached up to his eyes and rubbed them.

"Best find it, put it on. Sun'll be pounding you directly."

The boy still did not look up, but he moved toward the back of the wagon.

MacKinnon watched as the boy climbed in, and that was when he saw Honey, awake and alert, but not saddled.

Can I saddle her? he asked himself.

"We got tea, mister," a voice called out.

The next voice sounded harsher. "Florrie."

MacKinnon ignored the redhead and the blonde. He made himself take a step toward Honey, glancing at the saddle, tilted so it would dry, and the blanket on top of it, underside up so it could dry quicker, too.

The boy jumped down from the wagon, and MacKinnon gave the kid's hat a nod of approval. He looked around for his own hat, and saw it on the blanket, squashed, since he had used it as a pillow. Bending over to pick it up was out of the question. He pointed, and said: "Think you could hand me mine, Gary?"

"Sure."

Once MacKinnon managed to punch the hat into something of a shape, he pulled it on his head, and toyed with the stampede string until he had it to his liking. Or maybe, he realized, he was just stalling.

The two older girls were talking, making no attempt to keep what they were saying from MacKinnon.

"Can you saddle his horse?"

"I unsaddled it."

"You need help saddling her?"

"I can do it myself. I'm not an invalid."

"Then saddle her."

"Why don't he?"

"Because his ribs are broken, Florrie. Just saddle the horse as best you can."

"I don't guess he wants some tea."

"I could care less what he wants. What I want is for him to ride out of here. The sooner the better."

MacKinnon looked at the wagon, frowned, and studied the wheel. The iron rim had come loose and lay in the weeds. The wheel was leaning against the boulder that held the axle up. Two spokes were busted.

"I'm no wheelwright," MacKinnon declared as he touched the end of the axle with his hand. He began walking.

Honey was restless. The mule was blind indeed.

"What's he doing?" the redhead asked.

"I don't care."

"Maybe he's stealing our stuff."

"What would we have that's worth stealing?"

MacKinnon held out his hand, palm down, and let the mule take in his scent. He guessed the mule had to be pushing thirty years old.

"Good Sam MacKinnon," he said to himself, spit in the dust, and moved around the mule, keeping his hand on the animal's back until he had cleared the big animal.

He saw the kettle and the campfire. He moved to stand by the covered body.

That's when the blonde shouted: "Stay away from her!"

MacKinnon removed his hat, let it hang at his side, and bowed his head. He didn't pray. He wasn't sure he could remember how.

The blonde moved over beside him in an instant, and Gary and the redhead shifted closer hesitantly.

"We'll saddle your horse, mister," the older girl said. "And you can ride out of here. Do you understand?"

He did not answer.

"I mean for you to get." The girl was sure insistent.

He thought about kneeling down by the body, but quickly abandoned that thought. A pickaxe and shovel lay in the dirt. He toed the ground with his battered boot. His head shook in defeat. A moment later, hearing the girl's heavy breathing, MacKinnon turned back toward the mule.

"Do you hear what I'm telling you, mister?" the blonde said.

MacKinnon looked from the mule and took in the desert all around.

"I want you to ride out of here," the girl said.

"Later," MacKinnon told her.

CHAPTER EIGHTEEN

He heard one of the girls, or perhaps both, gasp when he finally knelt by the covered body. MacKinnon stiffened at the pain when he reached down and touched the tarp, but his ribs didn't hurt as badly as before. Maybe it was the way the blonde had wrapped his side. Probably he had grown accustomed to the discomfort.

"Listen to me," the blonde began.

"No." MacKinnon kept his voice even. "You listen to me. You got few options." He looked up at her. "You'll never bury her here. Not unless you have mining equipment and dynamite. Ground's like iron, especially this time of year. So we can put her in the back of the wagon, and burn it, but that'll mean you're stuck here till you can get another wagon." He paused. "Where did you say you were bound for?"

"I didn't."

He breathed in, breathed out, pulled his lower lip in over his teeth, and gave her what Slim Bradford used to call "Sam's look of contempt." He stared, and she stared back. He didn't say a word, just waited. She, he understood, wasn't about to give in.

"Pa wanted to try Shafter," Flossie sang out.

"Florrie!" The blonde whirled.

"He wants to help, Katie!" Florrie countered.

"He wants to rob us," Katie said.

"I'm no robber," MacKinnon said, and chuckled. *I'm still a born liar, but maybe that ain't no lie. Ask the folks at Bonito City. Ask Jace Martin. I've tried that line of work and decided that it don't fit me.* "I'm a thirty-a-month cowhand."

"Shafter's down . . . ," the redhead started to say, but Katie's glare caused her to bite her tongue.

"I know about Shafter, miss. It's about as tough a place as this here piece of . . ."—he sighed—"paradise." He began to push himself up, but the needle-like pain in his side sent him back to his haunches. He waited till the pain subsided before he opened his eyes. When he saw the boy moving toward him, MacKinnon grinned, and held out his hand.

"Reckon you can get me up again, Gary?"

The boy gave his sisters a quick look, but he didn't wait for their approval. He stepped closer, took MacKinnon's hand in both of his, and began moving backward like a plow horse. MacKinnon's legs pushed him forward, and he stood, chest heaving, waiting for the torment in his side to settle into something he could manage.

"There ought to be people traveling on this road, heading one way or the other," MacKinnon said, then paused for a few minutes of thought.

"One of you bring Honey." He nodded at the sorrel.

"You're leaving . . . ," Katie said.

MacKinnon wasn't sure if she were asking or telling, not that it mattered. He nodded to the south. "We'll use my horse to bring your mother over to that little rise, put her against it. Collapse the sand down on top of her. I can pry off a chunk of tailgate from your wagon, and I'll carve a marker for her." His head shook as memories arose. "Seen that done for a couple of cowhands I rode with."

He looked around and shook his head. "It's not a bad spot, really. Don't look like much, maybe, but those cactus will bloom after a monsoon. And it's peaceful. Rains won't wash her away, like they might if we took her to the arroyo. I reckon I can get enough dirt down to keep the critters away from her."

MacKinnon made eye contact with Katie. "It's not a cemetery. Not a churchyard. But you need to get her under the ground. And then we need to figure out how to get you to . . ."

"We?" she said with bitterness.

He shrugged. "Roswell's on the way to Shafter. I can get you that far."

"Maybe we don't want to go to Shafter."

"That's your business," he told her. "But Roswell's something of a town. You can get to El Paso or Fort Davis down south. Or Mesilla or Lincoln or Socorro to the west. Or Puerto de Luna or Las Vegas or Santa Fe up north. You can catch the railroad in El Paso or points east. Go anywhere you want to."

"We don't need your help."

"Yes," he said, "you do. Besides, I owe you." He gently rubbed his ribs. "And you're stuck with me. I'm your . . ."—he had to let out a sigh as he shook his head—"good Samaritan. That's me, you see. Good Sam MacKinnon."

MacKinnon found adequate harness and rope in the wagon. He threaded some underneath the tarp. The body wrapped with the blankets felt incredibly light, but it was a woman who had been consumed by consumption, so that did not surprise him. The blonde, Katie, helped, and MacKinnon tied the rope securely around the dead woman's midsection. They did this again around her upper body, her feet, and just above the head.

It was far from a pine box, but MacKinnon had seen men buried with nothing but a bedroll for a coffin, and sometimes less than that.

The siblings did not question what MacKinnon was doing. Maybe they thought it was the closest thing to a coffin he could come up with. But MacKinnon's main concern was pulling the body a hundred and fifty yards or so across the desert floor. Getting a corpse onto the back of Honey or the blind mule would be practically impossible, especially with MacKinnon's bum ribs, and the increasing smell of the decaying woman. MacKinnon figured he'd have a hard enough time just having Honey pull the body that distance.

Satisfied as he would ever be, MacKinnon let the children fetch Honey while he rigged a rope harness through some holes he had punched in the bottom tarp. When the children brought Honey over, MacKinnon held his breath. The wind blew, and maybe that relaxed the mare. He helped back the horse up about as close to the body as he dared, and grabbed the rope and gave it a few quick dallies around the saddle horn.

"All right," he said, and he took the reins, and walked toward the small knoll less than two hundred yards south.

He did not look behind him, but focused on the knoll, weaving around cactus and feeling the sun's heat. His ribs ached, his throat turned dry, but Honey never gave him any trouble. They made it to the knoll, and MacKinnon stopped to look back.

After a nod of approval, he brought the reins over the sorrel's head, rubbed her neck, and draped the reins below her mane. Quickly, he removed the rope and found the boy.

"Gary," he called, "come over here and keep my horse company!"

"Go ahead," Katie told her brother. "And be careful."

When Gary was next to him, MacKinnon instructed: "Just rub her neck, and take hold of the reins to make sure she don't bolt. She's been good so far, but Honey's notional. We don't want her to leave us afoot."

MacKinnon moved to the body and knelt to unthread the rope as Katie and Florrie walked over. He tossed the rope to the redhead, saying: "Coil that up if you would, Miss Florrie. Rope might come in handy."

Still on his knees, he gripped the canvas tarp and dragged the body closer to the side of the little hill. That little bit of effort gave him more fits than he expected. He found himself sweating, and his ribs either wanted to push through his skin or pierce his innards. He wasn't exactly sure which. He waited until his breathing stopped sounding so ragged, pushed his hat off his head, and blinked until he could see the girls.

Katie held the shovel and the pickaxe. She had carried the tools all the way from the campsite. MacKinnon hadn't even thought about that. Florrie had finished coiling the rope and was staring at him.

He tried to stand, couldn't. Watching him, Katie sighed, lowered the tools to the ground, and came to him. She extended both hands, and he sighed as he accepted her help, yelling out in pain as she brought him to his feet.

"Are you all right?" Florrie asked.

"Getting . . . there," he said between gasps.

Katie had already moved to her mother's feet, and was dragging that part of the body closer to the slight overhang. She looked up. "Is this good enough?"

MacKinnon nodded.

"Well?" Katie asked. "What do we do next?"

He hesitated. "You might want to walk back to camp. I can do the rest." Funerals were one thing. But watching MacKinnon bury their mother— if you could call what he planned on doing a burial—didn't seem proper.

"How do you plan on doing that?" Katie asked. She walked right past him, took the reins from Gary's hands, and led the horse back to the wrapped body. "You can't even climb into the saddle."

"I can," said Florrie, who tentatively approached the horse.

"No," MacKinnon said.

He felt their stares. "You use those tools." He nodded at the pickaxe and shovel. "Just start jamming them into the side here." Another nod. "Loosen up the ground. I'll get into the saddle."

"I can ride," Florrie told him.

He tried to smile. "I bet you can. I *know* you can. But this is ticklish. There's a chance Honey falls. You don't want to have this mare roll over you."

"Maybe," Florrie said, "we don't want her to roll over you, either."

His smile felt genuine. "Well, I do appreciate that, Miss Florrie. And I'll do my dam- . . . I'll do my best to keep that from happening."

He took the reins, and pulled the horse to the other side of the hill. There, he found a spot where he could climb a few feet up the knoll. He managed to stick his left foot into the stirrup, and somehow swung into the saddle without passing out from the pain.

Of course, that was the easy part.

CHAPTER NINETEEN

While the girls worked the earth with pick-axe and shovel, MacKinnon took a quick swallow from his canteen. Then he held the canteen out to Gary. The boy shook his head. MacKinnon lowered his and held the canteen out farther.

When the five-year-old hesitated, MacKinnon said: "It's hot. And the sun'll dry you up if you don't drink water." He shook the canteen slightly, but even that caused him to grimace. "Drink," he said. "Then take some to your sisters."

The boy obeyed, and, after he had a mouthful, he stepped away from the horse and moved toward his sisters, the gravediggers.

"That should be good enough," MacKinnon said to the girls, as he gathered the reins. "Have some water. Stay back . . . I don't know, thirty feet or so."

MacKinnon pressed his legs against the mare. Clucking his tongue, he moved Honey toward the mound. Once they reached it, near the body's feet, MacKinnon leaned toward the sorrel's neck, and kicked hard.

"Up," he said, and gave another kick as he gripped the reins tightly. "Up. Up. Up."

The horse leaped up. MacKinnon cringed. He

kept kicking. The mare snorted, lunged, as gravel, sand, and stones began cascading underneath Honey's forefeet. The horse was going higher, and now her rear feet smashed into the hillside. MacKinnon bit back the pain, and let Honey climb, climb, climb. The hillock maybe rose five feet off the desert plain, but it felt like he was climbing up those mountains south of Bonito City. They reached the top, and MacKinnon heard the dirt tumbling behind him. He let Honey step a few more feet before he pulled the reins, drawing in a shallow breath.

The knoll stretched maybe four more feet.

MacKinnon glanced to his left and right, and decided he had enough room to turn Honey around. Once he accomplished that, he wiped the sweat off his brow before nudging the mare back toward where she had just climbed. Again, he reined her up, stood in the stirrups, and looked below.

The body was covered up to her knees. How deep, MacKinnon couldn't guess, but at least that much had worked.

After settling back into the saddle, MacKinnon's eyes sought Gary, Florrie, and Katie. He couldn't see their faces clearly, and probably he didn't want to. How would he have felt had he watched the burial of his own mother at their age? Especially had she been buried this way. The kids, he had to admit, were strong.

"All right," he told the mare. "Let's try it this way."

He brought the horse down just below the top of the gentle rise, and kicked her as she moved six feet, then let her leap to the ground.

That gave him a sound jar, but he had been expecting it, and although he almost gagged up the water he had swallowed earlier, he didn't throw up, and he kept his seat. Not letting the horse relax, MacKinnon turned her around and rode up the knoll closer to the dead mother's head. Honey churned, snorted, and kicked, and again more sand and gravel rolled below. They stopped just long enough on the top to turn around and return to the desert floor. Again. Once more. Again. Twice more. MacKinnon knew he had played this hand as long as he cared to. He felt exhausted. Honey labored for breath, and the way she responded to the reins and his heels, he figured she was finished with this bit of business. Besides, that little rise held just so much dirt, and the last two treks up that mound had felt dicey. Honey had barely kept her footing. MacKinnon had just managed to keep from being dusted.

He leaned forward and rubbed the horse's neck. "Good girl," he whispered. "Good girl." He reached for the canteen, only to remember that the kids had it. MacKinnon straightened in the saddle, pulled his hat off his back, and waved it at the two girls and boy. His mouth opened, but his throat was too dry and his tongue too swollen to speak.

They understood, though, and began moving back toward the knoll.

Now MacKinnon twisted in the saddle and saw what he had done.

Few would call it a proper grave. But it was a start.

He considered staying in the saddle, but decided it wouldn't be right. Not at a funeral. So he gradually made himself step to the ground. He led the horse to the side of the knoll, and directed the two girls to flatten the dirt with shovel and pickaxe. When they were finished, he walked Honey over the mound.

"Back in those olden times," he told the children, "on the overland trails and such, they'd do this. It'll make it harder . . ." He stopped. The children didn't need to know everything. He figured Katie, the oldest understood, but maybe all three did.

Anyway, the wolves and coyotes would not likely disturb the woman. The mother could rest in peace. Maybe the kids could find some peace, too.

Florrie sang. The girl had the voice of an angel. MacKinnon couldn't recall the name of the hymn. The boy sobbed a bit, and Katie kept brushing at her eyes. MacKinnon kept his head bowed, hat in his left hand, reins in his right.

"We should pray," Florrie said when she had finished the song.

"Yeah," Katie said. She sniffed, sighed, and began: "Dear Lord . . ." A long silence followed.

MacKinnon wondered if the girl would continue. If she didn't, he worried he would have to come up with some words, and a long time had passed since he had been to a camp meeting or church social.

"We thank you for our mother, Heavenly Father," Katie picked up, and MacKinnon felt the pressure lift off his shoulders. "We thank you for her life, for her love."

Another long minute or two with nothing to hear but the wind, Gary's sobs, and the swishing of Honey's tail.

"She never had an easy life, God. We hope you find your way to give her what she deserved now. Because . . ."

MacKinnon waited.

"Because she never lost her faith. Maybe we didn't go to church as often as you'd have liked. Probably she wanted to go more than she did. And you know what happened to her Bible. But whoever paid Truluck for it might have gotten some good use . . ."

"Katie," Florrie said.

"Forgive me," Katie said. "We loved our

185

mother, God. Our mother loved us. She loved everybody, whether they deserved her love or not. And . . ."

MacKinnon pursed his lips. This silence seemed to be lasting an eternity.

"Give her peace, God. Give her love. We know she'll watch after us, and tell her we'll do the best we can. We thank you for what little time we had with her. We . . . we . . . we thank you for . . . for sending . . . this . . . this . . . good . . . Samaritan . . . to help us. We ask you to bless him, too."

MacKinnon shifted his feet. He felt like a louse.

"Heavenly Father, now let us commend the soul of Margaret Anne Roberts Callahan Truluck to you. Your will be done. I guess . . . this is a pretty place. Ma came to love the desert. Maybe the desert gave her more years than she'd have had back in Kansas. She loved when the cactus bloomed. There's plenty of cactus here. Amen."

When they returned to the wagon, MacKinnon watered both the horse and mule, before looking for a hammer. Once he found it, he gripped his ribs with his right hand and used the left to knock off part of the wagon's tailgate. He grabbed a knife, and gently lowered himself until he was leaning against the front wagon wheel still on the Studebaker.

Curious, Katie walked to the wagon and stood over him.

Ignoring her, MacKinnon stuck the point of the butcher knife into the wood.

"Margaret," he said. "That was your mother's name, right?"

"Yeah."

MacKinnon nodded. "That'd be M-a- . . . ?"

"M-a-r-g-a-r-e-t," she answered, adding as she stepped closer: "I can do that."

"I know you can. But you might think about getting some tea for you brother and sister." He turned his head toward the saddlebags. "There's some jerky in the left bag. And a little bit of coffee. Not much, but enough for something stronger than the tea."

"All right." She looked uncomfortable. "I don't know the year she was born." She drew in a deep breath and exhaled. "I don't know much about her, really."

"Don't think I knew much about my ma, neither," he said, and traced a letter **M** in the wood.

"What was her full name?" he asked. "I know it was a mouthful."

"Margaret Anne Roberts Callahan Truluck." She let out a slight laugh. "That won't fit on that board, mister."

He nodded. "Won't fit on the whole wagon . . . especially how I carve." He made himself look up. She had been crying. He could see that in her eyes. She wanted to cry some more, but she was the oldest, which meant she had to be the strong one.

"You want me to just make it Truluck?" He remembered how the boy had said that the sisters had a different last name because they had had a different father. "Or Callahan?"

"Truluck's shorter," Katie said.

Their eyes held.

"She married him. She stuck with him, flaws and all." Her Adam's apple bobbed. "I guess she even loved him."

"So that's T-r-u-e- . . . ," he started.

"No 'e'," she told him, and spelled out the name.

"I can make it Margaret C. Truluck," he suggested.

"It doesn't really matter," she said. "Does it?"

He waited.

"Dry as it is here. Wood on the wagon's already dried out. The wind and rain. The animals. That marker you're trying to make will get weathered away, blown over, washed away, the words faded . . . maybe before we even reach Roswell."

He recollected the cowboys he had helped bury. The boss hadn't wasted wood or time to put up a marker over their graves. Just a rock, under which he had placed their spurs and their names written in pencil on a piece of paper.

"It's not how you're buried," he told her. "Or where."

"Yeah," Katie said. I'll make you some coffee."

He took his time. When Katie had spelled her mother's name, he had written it in the sand on his right. He made sure not to shift and wipe away the letters accidentally. She had brought him coffee, and even some of his own jerky. The coffee, to his surprise, tasted fine. It refreshed him. Revitalized him.

Pressing the piece of wood on his thighs, he worked the butcher knife, carving the letters as deep and wide as he could, so they'd last for a while. When he heard footsteps, he drew the blade across the wood once more before looking up. Katie was staring at him, but MacKinnon looked beyond her, surprised to see how low the sun was. After placing the knife at his side, he held up the plank from the old wagon.

Margaret
Callahan
Truluck
Beloved Mother
Died 1885
RIP

Her lips parted as she stared at him in wonder. He saw the tears begin to well. She whispered: "My . . . goodness. . . ."

He shifted his legs in discomfort and looked

down at his feet. He had guessed at the spelling of beloved.

"Goodness gracious."

MacKinnon looked up and saw Florrie standing next to her sister. When next Gary came over and studied the rough piece of wood, he asked: "What's it say?"

Katie told him.

"We gonna put it up over the grave?" Gary asked.

They did. Without a word. The sun began sinking as they walked back to the wagon. There must have been dust blowing across the desert to the west, because the orange, red, and purple of the sunset seemed brighter, more intense than normal.

"Look!" Gary pointed. "That's pretty."

"It's beautiful," Florrie said, and began to cry. "God's welcoming Ma to Heaven." She took her brother's hand, and they walked away to admire the beauty.

MacKinnon moved to the fire, managed to squat, and poured himself another cup of coffee. He glanced up to find Katie staring down at him.

"You want some?" he asked.

"No," she said. And waited.

He decided he'd just sit for a bit, until he could find the will to try to stand. She still stared at him, and he looked at her again.

"Thank you," Katie told him.

CHAPTER TWENTY

He stood over the busted wheel. Although two spokes had split apart, MacKinnon thought he might be able to fix that, or at least come up with a repair that could possibly get them to Roswell. The metal tire, however, had separated from the wheel. That caused MacKinnon to think back to the time when they were driving a small herd to Magdalena, before it was actually called Magdalena. The wooden tire had shrunk because of the heat, and the metal tire had fallen off. MacKinnon had been ordered to help the cookie—as sorry a belly-cheater as MacKinnon had ever known—who had told him: "You're about as good a wheelwright as you is a cowpuncher, boy."

MacKinnon sneezed suddenly as he recalled that time. He rocked back on his heels, knees bent, his left hand gripping his bad ribs as tears of pain welled up in his eyes.

Gary stuck his head around the corner of the wagon. "Are you all right, Mister MacKinnon?"

He managed to lift his head, and smile at the boy. His head bobbed, and he raised his right hand toward the five-year-old.

"Want to help me up, Gary?" he muttered.

The boy hesitated.

"You know how good you are at helping me up, Gary." MacKinnon made himself smile, and Gary returned it as he moved closer.

Once he was standing and back to breathing regularly, MacKinnon told Gary: "I got a chore for you." Out of the corner of his eye, he caught Florrie and Katie standing by the wagon.

"Got chores for all of you," he said.

Gary dragged the dead creosote bushes to the fire. Florrie rolled the wagon rim, and Katie dragged the wheel. When MacKinnon offered to help, she shooed him away.

"Is that it?" the blonde asked, brushing her bangs off her forehead.

MacKinnon frowned. "I think we'll need more wood."

"There's not much left," Katie said. "And if this doesn't work . . ."

"It'll work," he assured her, but he was far from confident in his ability to fix a busted wheel. "Get the hatchet," he said, and when the boy ran to the wagon, MacKinnon smiled. "Whoa, Gary. Let one of your sisters do the chopping." The last thing he needed was for the boy to whack off a toe or a finger. "I got a special job for you."

The boy frowned, but soon beamed as he came back to MacKinnon. Katie found the hatchet, and MacKinnon said: "Chop up a few bushes. Wood'll be green. But it'll burn." He rubbed the top of the boy's hair. "Gary . . ."—he nodded at his saddle—"you see those strips of rawhide dangling behind the cantle?"

"Yes, sir."

"Cut about two . . . no, four of them." That would leave him two to attach to his bedroll. "Cut them as close to the saddle as you can." He pulled out his pocket knife, and opened the blade. "With this. Careful. It's sharper than a barber's razor." Which it wasn't. MacKinnon was lousy at keeping the edge on a blade.

Katie hacked at creosote, and Florrie oversaw her brother's job as MacKinnon settled himself onto the ground by the wheel.

When Gary brought over the strips of rawhide, MacKinnon nodded his approval. The boy started to return the knife, but MacKinnon shook his head. "That's your payment, son. Every boy ought to have a knife. Only you got to promise me you'll be careful with it."

"Oh, boy!" Gary grinned.

Florrie didn't. "Katie's not going to like this one bit. I don't like it, either."

"He'll be fine. He's careful."

"Till he cuts his hand off."

MacKinnon shook his head. "Then he'll learn just like Wade Stuart learned. He cut his left hand off once, but, by thunder, he learned his lesson. Never cut the right one off. Though he did chop off a toe with an axe. But just one."

Florrie's mouth hung open.

MacKinnon realized the story sounded a lot funnier in a bunkhouse or grog shop.

Florrie made a face, and started toward her sister, maybe to help chop up the bush, but more than likely to squeal on MacKinnon's latest transgression.

"Wait up!" he called.

The redhead sighed and looked back. He pointed at the wheel. "I got a chore for you, too, little lady."

"All right," MacKinnon told the girl several minutes later. "Gary and I will pull the spoke as close together as we can. When I say so, you tie that rawhide string as tight as you can. And I mean you have to pull that leather hard and strong . . . tight. Then come back under and over and give it another hard tie. Think you can do that, Florrie?"

"I'm stronger than I look," she said.

"Good," MacKinnon said. "Good. You ready, Gary?"

"Ready."

MacKinnon drew in a painful breath, set his jaw, tightened his hold on the spoke, and prayed that they didn't pull the wood all the way off or split it in two. "Pull, Gary, pull."

MacKinnon ignored the tearing pain in his right side, and when the pieces seemed to line up, he managed to grunt: "Now, Florrie." The girl's small hands placed the leather string between MacKinnon's and Gary's hands. She crossed the leather, slipped one end under the other, and pulled hard. The knot tightened against the wood, and she tugged till the leather seemed about to cut into the dried spoke. With that, she threaded the leather lace again, and repeated the process.

"Think you got enough left in you to make one more pass?" MacKinnon asked tightly.

"Maybe."

She did, and when she tied the third knot, MacKinnon gave her a nod and another order. "Tie it again. Till there's not enough length to make another knot."

When she was done, MacKinnon and Gary moved away, and let Florrie use another piece of leather a few inches down.

"That's good," MacKinnon said. "Now let's fix that other one."

That took slightly less time, and when MacKinnon pushed himself away from the wheel, Florrie stood, frowning at the work she had done. "That's not going to hold, Mister MacKinnon," she said. "It'll be just like my shoelaces."

"Maybe," MacKinnon said. He pulled his canteen over. "But your laces ain't leather." He opened the container, and poured water over the leather strips.

"What are you doing?" Katie yelled, dropping the creosote she was carrying as she ran to the trio. "We don't have water to waste like that," she scolded.

He nodded at the soaking spokes as he put the stopper back on the canteen. "Sun'll dry out the leather, and the leather will shrink. It'll hold those spokes together better than anything else we had on hand."

Katie frowned, but she seemed to accept MacKinnon's theory.

God, you'll be doing me a mighty big favor if you let this work, MacKinnon thought.

Once the kindling caught fire from the coals, MacKinnon let Florrie and Gary feed the flames with larger pieces of wood, and when the fire seemed big enough, he and Katie began dragging the big pieces of creosote into the fire.

That's what he was doing when he heard the jingling of a harness and the clattering of hoofs.

"Stagecoach!" he shouted, and moved away from the fire and to the side of the road. Despite the discomfort in his ribs, he was so filled with joy, he felt like screaming and dancing as he raised his hat and began waving it over his head.

Katie quickly joined him, moving her arms about like a pinwheel.

White dust sailed behind the mud wagon as the jehu worked the whip, urging the six mules galloping down the road.

"Halloooo!" MacKinnon shouted joyously.

The messenger leaned forward. The whip snapped again.

Florrie and Gary were jumping up and down a few feet from Katie and MacKinnon.

But the stagecoach kept thundering toward the east, toward Roswell.

MacKinnon stopped waving his hat as he shouted: "Hey there. Stop! We need some help. Stop! Stop! Help us!"

He watched as the messenger picked up his shotgun while the driver practically stood in the box, lines in his hands, cursing the mules and urging them onward.

MacKinnon unleashed every piece of blasphemy, every bit of profanity he could recall as the stagecoach raced past. He stepped onto the road, staring at the trailing dust—for now that was all he could see of the mud wagon—and he raised his fist and directed more profanities at the stupid messenger and the coward of a driver.

He could have done that as long as he could stand, but when he looked at the others, he drew in a deep breath. Florrie was on her knees, sobbing, and Gary had this strange look on his face. Katie simply seemed resigned. He saw the fire, though, and he moved to it.

Florrie looked up, sobbing: "Why didn't they stop?"

"Schedule to keep," MacKinnon said. "Figured

we were road agents. Who knows? It don't matter."

"We're never getting out of here," she moaned.

"Chins up," he said. "We don't need that stagecoach. We don't need nobody. We'll do this ourselves. Come here. All of you."

None budged.

He let loose more curses, then: "Don't you dare feel sorry for yourselves. We're getting out of this furnace. But that means we've got work to do. Help me." He started to bend, but the pain forced him back up. "Get this tire on that fire. Now. Quick. While the flames are still hot."

"Move!" he thundered, and watched all three of them jump.

While the fire crackled and the iron tire got hotter and hotter, MacKinnon and the others busied themselves. They cut up the remainder of Tommy Truluck's clothes. Using the least amount of water they dared, Gary and Florrie got the strips wet and then laid them onto the bottom of the wooden wheel, while Katie tacked the pieces on. It was up to MacKinnon to rotate the wheel until the cloth covered the entire wheel.

The fire had started to die down, and MacKinnon stood over it, staring at the red-hot tire.

"This is the hard part," he said. "Watch your fingers. Watch your clothes and your toes."

Grunting and grimacing while trying his best to ignore the searing heat on his fingers, knuckles, and the backs of his hand, MacKinnon used both hands to lift the wheel rim with the hammer's handle. At the same time, Katie lifted with a steel carpenter's square, the L-shape giving her more leverage than a hammer. MacKinnon could see the tears in her eyes and the pain in her face as she lifted against the heat. The boy used a hayfork, and the younger girl a shovel, which at least protected them more from the heat. MacKinnon and Katie backed up. The tire slipped off the hammer, landed on the ground. He swore again, but picked it up before the others dropped their ends, then they all shifted the tire over the wooden wheel.

Quickly, he banged the tire with the hammer. The soaking cloth steamed from the red-hot metal, as MacKinnon continued swinging the hammer, ramming the tire over the wood. The others tried to help as best they could. The clinging rang out so loudly that the mule and horse snorted. Finally the tire fell into place, the cloth sizzling.

All four were soaked from sweat as they looked down at the tire.

"That stinks," Gary said.

MacKinnon grinned. "Smells better than hot biscuits to me," he said, nodding. "Y'all done good."

"You think it'll hold?" Katie asked.

He shrugged. "If the seal holds. It worked on the trail ten years back." Wiping his brow, he nodded at the wagon. "We'll let the tire cool, then put it on the axle." He pointed. "I'll need one of you to fetch that grease bucket. We'll need to grease that pretty good."

"I want to do that," Gary said.

"Of course you do." Katie rolled her eyes.

That made MacKinnon laugh. It felt good, too.

CHAPTER TWENTY-ONE

"I don't think Honey likes pulling this wagon," Gary said.

The boy sat on the seat between MacKinnon and Katie as the wagon crept along the road, the sun sinking behind the mountains at their backs. In the back of the wagon, Florrie sang "The Flying Trapeze"—she had a soothing voice, MacKinnon thought, remembering how his mother, who knew she was tone deaf, usually just hummed the tune.

"She don't like much of anything." MacKinnon flicked the lines. "But she's a pretty good cow pony."

The front wheel on Katie's side hit a hole, the wagon lurched and leaned, but the wheel held, and the relic kept moving eastward. Every hole they hit caused MacKinnon to cringe and bite his bottom lip. At this rate, he figured he would chew it off completely long before they ever saw Roswell.

"I'm glad that stagecoach didn't stop," the boy said.

"How come?"

"You'd be gone. You wouldn't have stayed with us. We'd be going back to some place, and you'd be heading to . . . wherever it is you're going. I'd miss you."

MacKinnon kept his eyes focused on Honey and the mule, but eventually he looked at the boy, who smiled. MacKinnon tried to think of something to say, but then his eyes moved past the boy and found Katie, who stared ahead at the empty land. When he looked back at Gary, he said: "Miss me? Ain't nobody ever missed me, Gary."

"I would," the boy said. "We all would."

"You'd miss my horse is what you mean." He reached over and ran his right hand roughly over the boy's head. "Ain't that right?"

"No," the boy said, trying to duck underneath MacKinnon's hand, but Sam MacKinnon could be persistent—at least until those blasted ribs of his did their thing again.

"You all right?" Gary asked.

MacKinnon nodded. "Yeah. But I still don't think you'd miss me."

"You're just saying that. I can tell. I'm five years old."

Katie kept looking at the road, but MacKinnon could tell she was smiling. Thinking quickly, he shoved the lines into the boy's hands. The boy took them in a panic.

"Ever drove a team before, Gary?" MacKinnon asked.

"No, sir." The boy tried to return the heavy lines to MacKinnon, who ignored them.

"Well, give her a whirl."

• • •

They camped in a clearing at a bend in the Río Hondo, which held a trickle of water before it dipped underground, not to emerge for miles.

"I'd boil the water before you drink it," he warned, and drew the Winchester from the scabbard.

"Where you going?" Gary asked.

"To see if I can't find us something to eat."

"Oh." The boy's frown quickly turned into a smile. "Can I come?"

"Didn't driving Honey and Bartholomew wear you out?"

"No, sir. It was fun. Doing fun chores don't make you tired."

"I'll try to remember that." He patted the kid's back. "But you ought to stay here. Snakes might start coming out, and I don't know this country too well. If I get lost, who'd come to find me if you was with me?"

"Oh." The boy shrugged. "Can I boil the water?"

Katie handed him a pot. "You have to get some first."

He took it and ran down the embankment. "Bring us back a deer!" he called out. "A big one."

"That might be hard for me to pack out." MacKinnon laughed and turned to Katie. "I'll be lucky to find a jack rabbit."

"Be careful," she told him.

• • •

He came back with sand in his boots, and ears, thirsty and tired, and his ribs hurting more than ever. He had found nothing to shoot at. On the other hand, he had found no horse tracks or any sign of Jace Martin, Nelson Bookbinder, or Charley The Trey. But he brought back prickly pears.

Florrie, Katie, and Gary stared at him as he deposited the purple pears and the green pads. He let them look, as he pulled on his gloves and went to work.

"They'll stick my tongue," Gary said.

Laughing, MacKinnon sliced off the ends of the pears, and tossed those into the fire. Holding the fruit between thumb and forefinger, he cut a line vertically, then slid his finger into the cut and pulled away the skin. This he tossed into the fire, as well. When he looked up, he grinned and popped the pear in his mouth.

"It don't hurt?"

"Kind of chewy. Like gum. But tasty." He might have been stretching the truth.

"Let me help." Katie sat beside him, telling Florrie to bring another knife and a couple of plates.

"Good," MacKinnon said, still chewing the pear. "You do these. I'll do the pads."

"You eat them, too?" Gary asked.

"You'll eat anything if you get hungry enough,

Gary. You want small pads," he explained to the boy. "At least, that's what the Mexican cook we had at the Seven-T-X told me. Not as many spines. Sap not as thick or foul. Can I borrow that knife I give you, Gary?"

He used the knife to pare what spines he could, then speared the bottom of the pad and held it over the fire, burning off the small, even invisible stickers. He asked Florrie for a bowl of water, and when she brought it, he soaked the pads, before slicing them long-ways. He was finished before Katie, so he moved closer and helped her.

As MacKinnon chewed on the cactus fruit by the fire, the boy ran back from the wagon where he had disappeared several minutes before. He slid to a stop at MacKinnon's side.

"It's not exactly roast beef and raspberry jam," MacKinnon was commenting to Florrie. He looked up at Gary and said: "What you got there?"

"A book." The boy shoved it toward MacKinnon. "Can you read it to us?"

MacKinnon laughed.

"Gary!" Florrie said.

"That's all right, Miss Florrie." He took the dime novel. "I can read."

"I didn't mean . . . ," the middle child said.

He laughed and looked at the gaudy cover. *"The Scalp-Hunters; or, Adventures Among the*

Trappers. Sounds kind of blood-and-thunder, don't it?"

"It's better than what she reads." He nodded at Katie.

MacKinnon looked at her. "What does she read?"

"Ma called it filth," Florrie said, and giggled. "Or trash."

"I see. I rode with a teen-aged boy west a ways, and he was always reading. Even in the saddle. Ever read *Alice in Wonderland*?"

All three shook their heads.

"Me, neither. Gene did, though. Read Shakespeare, too. But, me?" He waved Gary's book, saying: "This is what real folks read. Blood and thunder. And maybe it'll have enough trash and filth to entertain your big sister. Let's see what happens." He turned to the first page.

Squatting at the edge of the camp, rifle cradled in his arms, MacKinnon stared into the night. Katie walked from the wagon, past the campfire, and over to him.

"It was the first time I ever ate cactus," she said, and smiled. "The pads were pretty good. The pears, well . . ."

"The cook I knew made them like a jelly. That'd be a bit out of my ability."

"That was some story," she said, and sat down across from him.

He laughed. "I've read a passel of books like that."

"It's not Shakespeare."

"I wouldn't know, ma'am."

She remained silent for a few seconds before saying: "Me, either."

They laughed.

The wind blew, and she shivered.

"You ought to go by the fire, Miss Callahan."

Her eyes closed, and she let out a weary sigh. "I wish you wouldn't call me miss . . . or ma'am. My name's Katie."

"Sorry, ma'am."

She rose, and he did, too, clutching his ribs. "That wasn't a joke, miss . . . ma'- . . . aw . . . Katie. It's just . . ."

"Are you all right?"

"At least I didn't sneeze." With a grin, he sank back onto his haunches. "But you really should get back to the fire. I'll be along directly."

She did not go.

"I was wrong about you," she said.

Their eyes locked, and his jaw moved to the left, then the right, as he considered what he should say.

"No," he said, "Katie, you weren't."

She tested the word: "Sam . . ."

His shoulders sagged, and he shook his head sadly as he made himself look at her. "Katie, I was riding away. I would have left you, your brother, your sister, and your ma, had Honey not spooked. You best remember that."

"I think you would have ridden back."

He let out a mirthless chuckle and swore underneath his breath.

"You swear a lot."

"Yes, ma- . . . yep. I sure do."

"My mother made me wash my mouth out with soap."

He looked at her.

"More than once," she said.

MacKinnon found himself grinning. Soon Katie held up three fingers.

"You're joshing me."

"No, Sam, I'm not."

"Three times?"

"Ask Florrie. Gary's too young to remember the first two times, but he might recall the last time." She laughed. "It wasn't that long ago."

"What did you say?"

"Which time?"

He shrugged. "The last time."

Her lips parted, then closed. "I can't."

"Well, I understand."

Then, on her knees, she moved closer. He could smell her as she leaned forward, her dirty blonde hair brushing against the beard on his cheeks, and he felt her breath on his ear. She giggled, but finally whispered the word, and shifted back, glancing over her shoulder at the camp and the fire and her brother and sister. Still grinning, she looked back at Sam MacKinnon.

"Well?" she asked.

"If I'd said that, after Ma fed me lye soap, I'd've got a razor strop across my hide from Pa." MacKinnon dropped his head and swore softly. "I didn't mean to bring up your pa, Katie," he said.

"He wasn't my father," she said. She made herself smile again, and rose. "It's all right if I call you Sam?"

He shrugged. "Well, it beats what you said to your mother."

She laughed then, musically, and her eyes brightened. "I'll see you back at camp, Sam."

He watched her go, watched her longer than he should have, and, shifting his feet, tried to find a position that didn't hurt too much. He smiled, shook his head, frowning and wondering: *Would I have ridden back?*

Chapter Twenty-Two

"What does that sign say?" Four-Eyes Sherman, no longer having his glasses, asked as they trotted their horses into Roswell. His voice rose a couple of octaves. "Hey, is it the Fourth of July?"

"That was weeks ago, *amigo*," Chico Archuleta said. "This is not even my country, and I know that."

"Because you got drunk," Parker said.

Archuleta laughed. "But I get drunk almost every day, not just holidays, Mexican or one of your *norteamericano* reasons to have fun."

They were past the sign that stretched across the streets to find the buildings decorated with red, white, and blue bunting.

"But what did that sign say?" Sherman repeated, and waved behind him.

Another banner flapped in the wind at the far end of town.

"It's a stupid baseball game," Jace Martin said.

"Oh." Sherman's shoulders slouched in disappointment.

"But they'll be selling beer for a nickel." The kid grinned at the old man.

"And you, Harry, can drink all the lemonade you want," Archuleta said, and laughed when Parker pouted. "Free. Free. Free."

"Nickel beer?" Sherman asked.

Jace Martin had already turned his horse toward the hitching rail. "I think we can find something stronger than five-cent draught beers," he said, and swung off his horse in front of the Río Hondo Saloon. "And not have to wait till Saturday to cut the dust."

"This place might as well be Texas," Jace Martin complained as the bartender poured four whiskeys, although he eyed Harry Parker for all of two seconds before filling his glass.

"How's that?" The barkeep had short gray hair that stopped at the top of his ears. He wore an apron and the hang-dog look of a man with no ambition, no future, and could care less.

"It's not the end of the world," Martin said as he held up the glass to examine the quality of the rye. "But you can see it from here." He took a sip.

The barkeep waited.

Martin fished out a gold piece and laid it on the rough counter.

The barkeep was not impressed, but he asked: "You want me to leave the bottle?"

Martin was about to nod, when Harry Parker asked: "What's all the big fuss about this baseball game?" The hatless, sun-burned kid then laughed, took a healthy swallow, and coughed until his eyes watered. That brought a smile to

211

the bartender's lips. They drank in silence until Parker again brought up the game.

"It's a big to-do," the barkeep said. "Playing Engle."

Martin shook his head. "Oh, of course. Engle."

"It's a big game, mister." Martin's sarcasm riled the old barkeep. "They take their baseball seriously in Engle. Railroaders mostly. And you might find it hard to believe, but baseball's big here in Roswell."

Chico Archuleta chuckled and killed his whiskey. "I believe a *siesta* is big in this town." He helped himself to the bottle.

"Well, if you're here on Saturday, you'll see for yourselves." The barkeep had a full-blown case of civic pride. "People will come up from Seven Rivers and Eagle Draw."

Jace Martin did not even try to hide it when he rolled his eyes.

The barkeep picked up the bottle and returned it to the shelf that served as a backbar. He was talking, though, and that sheepish look had been replaced by a scowl. "Laugh all you want, boys, but come Saturday, this town'll be booming more than any of your mining camps to the west or Mesilla or Las Vegas or Santa Fe."

He stared at each man individually as he went through his speech.

"The railroad's brass are sporting men, and they place a lot of bets. Some of you fellows look like you've punched cattle, so you know how much pride a cowhand has. Those railroad bets are matched. Stagecoach pulled in from Las Cruces, full of folks who come here just for this game."

He waved his finger. "You boys drifted in from the west and south. I saw that. That means you come over *El Alto*, 'The Height', and I'm betting that you saw what we call *La Gara*, 'The Rag', because that's the poor side of town, where you'll find all that laundry hanging in the wind to dry." He nodded in another direction. "But over yonder. That's what we call *Barrio de Los Ricos*." He turned to Archuleta. "Tell your *amigos* what that means, buster."

Archuleta wet his lips and looked at Martin. "The Neighborhood of the Rich Folks."

"Indeed. Rich white folks is what they really mean." He stepped back. "You boys still thirsty?"

"I haven't asked for change," Jace Martin said. "Pour and talk."

The barkeep obliged. "We got a hundred folks in this town. They'll all be at that game in a few days. The boys from Engle are already here. They had some ball games in El Paso over the weekend. And some gamblers from El Paso came up with them."

He had everyone's attention now.

"Simon Hibler Town Field was erected last year from the winnings of this annual baseball stump match. So, yeah, this town ain't much to

look at right now, but fifty cents a head for adults
. . . say two hundred . . . and two bits for a kid . . .
put that around twenty-five . . . and it don't take a
schoolmarm who got through all his McGuffey's
READERs to figure out that this one day'll take
in a lot of money."

He stepped back to study the faces of the
strangers, and was satisfied with the impression
he had made.

"And that ain't even taking into account the
money I'll make on nickel beers, not to mention
all the whiskey I'll sell after and before the
game." He came back to the bar with the bottle.
"And the money they'll be holding at the front
gate for all the bets. Well, this ain't New Orleans
or Denver City on most days, but come Saturday,
it'll be right near close."

"This one's on the house, boys." He refilled
the glasses, and Jace Martin held his glass up
in a salute to the bartender before moving to an
empty table against the west wall.

"Let's split the money and light a shuck for
Texas," Four-Eyes Sherman said.

"Not yet." Jace Martin put his fingertips
together.

"We can't stay here," Parker whispered. "The
law . . ."

"I'm thinking we can make us some extra
money, boys," Martin said, and he grinned.

"Give that old fool at the bar something to tell the next dusty travelers. Get us mentioned in the Santa Fe newspaper. Maybe as far as Tucson or Fort Worth. Why are you looking at me that way, Chico?"

"*¡Es porque actúas como un loco y hablas como un loco!*" Chico Archuleta blurted out, and switched to English. "It is no good."

Martin leaned forward. "There will be more than one hundred dollars in that cash box, boys, once that baseball game gets started. And that's just for the tickets to the game. They'll also be holding money from all the bets. You heard that old codger."

Four-Eyes Sherman whistled, but Harry Parker shook his baked head.

"It don't seem worth the effort," the kid said. "Robbing a baseball game?"

"Jesse James robbed the Kansas City Fair," Martin reminded him.

"I recollect that," Four-Eyes Sherman said. "We might get writ up just like that one done."

"And get killed just like Jesse," Harry Parker added.

The old man snorted. "Like ten years later, kid. I'm all for it. Get me a new pair of glasses with that kind of money."

"Keep your voice down," Martin said. "We wait here till that game, ride over, and relieve them of their take from the tickets and the bets." Martin

215

turned to Archuleta. "Am I still talking crazy?"

"Have you forgotten about who we left out there?" Archuleta reminded him.

"Not at all, Chico. But Nelson Bookbinder's dried up and blown away by now. We might be bones, too, if we hadn't come across that water hole the evening after we stole his horses. And if Bookbinder's not dead, he will be soon. He's got no water. He's got no horses. And if he somehow finds that same water hole we lucked upon, good for him. We'll be loping into Texas by the time he could get here."

"Our horses are played out," Archuleta pointed out.

Martin nodded. "I know. I also know the gent who runs the livery in this town. I'm fairly certain we can make a trade."

"There's a lawman in this town," Parker said. "I saw the office."

"Yeah. But we left a much tougher law dog out in that furnace," Martin said. He nodded toward the dust blowing down the street. "We trade our horses. Sleep in the wagon yard. Rest up. Leave our guns in town and just take in all the wonders Roswell has to offer. There's a gal . . ." He chuckled. "We get new clothes. A bath. A shave. See what else we can find that'll pass the time in Roswell. Sleep in. Eat our fill of enchiladas and beef. On Saturday, when that ball game has started, we make our play. Then we ride to

Texas. Then we split our haul and go our merry way."

"And what if Charley The Trey shows up?" Parker asked.

Martin shrugged. "So what? He doesn't know us. And if he thinks he does, we'll just kill him."

CHAPTER TWENTY-THREE

Driving the wagon, MacKinnon debated if he should make camp now, or see if the team could take them one mile farther, maybe two. Honey and Bartholomew made a pretty good team, all things considered. He turned back, found the sun, and was amazed at how red and orange it looked. The wind blew harder, and dust devils popped up alongside the road they had passed. The wind and the sun did not mean a thing to MacKinnon right now. What concerned him was how far he could go today.

He figured the longer they traveled, the closer to Roswell he got. The closer to Roswell, the closer he was to Texas, or, maybe, Jace Martin, though he had pretty much given up on ever finding Martin. Getting away from the territorial law, and Charley The Trey, had become his priority.

At least, he kept trying to tell himself that.

"Here," came a voice.

He straightened back around, and saw the canteen Katie held toward him.

"I'm all right," he said, and the words hurt his throat.

The canteen held firm. So did Katie's face.

In the bed of the driver's box, Gary slept.

"You're relentless," MacKinnon said, and took the canteen with his right hand, keeping the leather lines in his left.

"Look who's talking," Katie said.

They smiled.

The water, tepid, not very good, did wonders on his tongue and throat, and he found himself taking one extra sip before returning the canteen to Katie.

"You should have some, too," he told her.

With a nod, she drank. A gust of wind caused her to turn her head.

When she turned back, she found MacKinnon moving the lines toward her. "Take these," he said, and when she did, he brought up the Winchester carbine.

His face had turned hard again, his mouth set, and his eyes did not blink, even with the wind and sand, as he looked to the southeast, well off the road.

It took her a moment before she found the men. Four of them. Two waving their arms over their heads, while they ran. One walking. One standing still. The sinking sun reflected off buckles and spurs—and weapons.

"Who could they be?" she asked.

His head shook. He wet his lips, considering his options.

She glanced at the strangers again. Judging distance had never ranked among her strengths.

If they were yelling, their voices were not reaching them, but the wind had changed course, now blowing from the north. She could make out a few things, though.

"They have rifles," she said.

MacKinnon nodded.

"Can we outrun them?" she asked.

"Maybe." He kept staring at the men.

"Oh," Katie said suddenly. "Oh, my." She stared to the north, her mouth open for a moment, and then she added: "What is that?"

MacKinnon looked, frowned, and said: "Dust cloud."

"It's gigantic!" shouted Florrie, who had just popped her head through the opening. "I've never seen anything like it."

On the floor of the box, Gary turned over, mumbling something as he started to wake up.

Taking the lines from Katie, MacKinnon rose to his feet, whipped the leather furiously, and Honey and the blind mule responded. They bounced along for about fifty yards as MacKinnon watched the men in the desert.

"Hiya!" he shouted to the animals, considering using the quirt.

"Stay down there, Gary," Katie told her brother, and she clutched the seat for a good hold. Florrie moved back inside the wagon.

The wind blew harder. The sand felt like birdshot.

Suddenly, MacKinnon fell back into the seat, pulling hard on the lines, bringing the wagon to a stop. He jerked his bandanna up to cover his mouth and nose, and helped Gary up onto the bench.

"Into the back, Gary," he said, and did not wait for the sleepy boy to respond. He scooped the kid up and pushed him into the opening. "Florrie, take your brother."

Empty-handed, he grabbed the reins, had Honey and Bartholomew turn the wagon so that its back faced the coming sandstorm. "Get back there," he ordered Katie. "Pull down that canvas, tie it down as tight as you can."

"What about Bartholomew?" she asked. "Or your mare?"

He had to shout over the rising wind. "They'll be all right. Backs to the wind." He jerked the brake, and leaped over the side, bringing the Winchester with him.

"Sam!" she cried.

He stopped, and met her eyes. "You don't know them!" she yelled over the fury. Then so soft that he could barely understand her over the popping of the canvas covering and the snorts and stamps from the two animals. "Or do you?"

"I can't leave them in this!" He turned, lowered his head, held the hat on his head with his free hand, and moved toward the four men. A hundred yards into the desert, he stopped.

Those four men, staggering in the wind, trying to reach him, were not Chico Archuleta, Four-Eyes Sherman, the kid Parker, and Jace Martin. That much he knew. Jace Martin might have sent two men running ahead, but he wouldn't show himself until he knew he had the upper hand.

Still, MacKinnon hefted the rifle, felt the wind blasting his neck, and tried to make out whether he knew the identity of the men. He started waving the rifle as best as he could in the wind.

"Over here! Over here! Over here!"

He could barely see them now, so he started to turn, the sand stinging his cheeks. But at least he could see the wagon. For right now. Looking back, he eared back the hammer, butted the stock against his thigh, and fired a round into the air. Then he jacked the lever. He listened, keeping his head lowered, hoping his hat wouldn't be swept off. He had always favored snug hats, so only the hat brim bent. When he heard nothing, he squeezed the trigger again.

I sure hope those boys don't think I'm shooting at them, he thought. *But it'd take a lucky shot to hit me if they do.*

This time, he thought he heard something in response. A faint pop. Maybe. It could have been his imagination. He turned around to find the wagon, now just a misty outline, and he guessed the distance before the wind and sand made him turn back. He tried to spit out the sand collecting in his mouth—and then his hat was gone. Swearing, he lowered his head even more, worked the lever, and fired another round that the wind appeared to choke off instantly.

This time, he could hear the pop of a pistol in return. At least it sounded like a handgun, but with all this howling wind, it might have been a battleship's deck gun.

"Over here!" he shouted, and squeezed off another shot.

The reply came quicker, maybe closer. He wondered how many shells he had left. Again, he levered a cartridge into the carbine, and shot off another round.

"Over here!" he yelled.

He heard an answering shot, and something that sounded like a man's voice. They were close, he thought. He wanted to look back, but refused. The Winchester barked again. The pistol sent its echo a few seconds later.

"I'm over here!" MacKinnon yelled.

"Where?" came a faint cry.

Quickly, MacKinnon snapped off another shot, but he did not wait for an answer. He chambered a new round, and touched the trigger. Jacked the lever. Fired. And did this twice more.

"Here!" he screamed. "Here I am! I'm over here!"

The party of four did not answer with a bullet

in the air. That made MacKinnon worry, and he cocked the .38-40, but held his fire. Nor did he lower the hammer. *Maybe they're out of bullets. Maybe I was wrong. Maybe that's Jace, after all.* He dropped to a knee, just to be safe, or at the least to feel a tad safer. "Here!" he called out. There was no answer. MacKinnon frowned.

But then he could make out something. It wasn't gunfire.

"My dog did bark . . ." That was it. The rushing wind drowned out whatever else was said. But then a moment later, he heard: ". . . up dat tree . . ." But that, too, died.

He furrowed his brow, stifled a cough, and considered touching off one more round.

Then he understood something, just a few words—"Oh, carve dat possum, carve . . ." They were lyrics from an old minstrel tune some of the boys had sung from time to time on a couple of the outfits he'd worked for.

If they wanted to kill me, he thought, *they wouldn't be singing. Besides, even though rifle shots might be louder, they're sporadic. Singing a song don't let up.*

The song, as best as he could remember was called something like "Carve That Possum." He shook his head. He didn't know the lyrics, but he knew a different song, so he wet his lips, and sang out, in what no one would consider a tune.

> Once me and Lem Briggs and old Bill Brown,
> We took us a load of corn to town.
> My old Jim dog, the ornery cuss,
> He just naturally followed us.

No response except the blasting of sand. MacKinnon tried again:

> As we drove past the general store,
> A passel of yaps came out the door.
> Old Jim stopped to smell of a box,
> They shot at him a bunch of rocks.

This time, he heard what sounded like at least two men singing, who sounded as awful as he did.

> Carve dat possum, carve dat possum, children,
> Carve dat possum, carve him to the heart;
> Oh, carve dat possum,
> carve dat possum, children,
> Carve dat possum, carve him to the heart.

That was the chorus, so MacKinnon shouted more than sang the chorus to his song.

> Every time I go to town,
> The boys keep kicking my dog around.
> It makes no difference if he is a hound,
> They gotta quit kicking my dog around.

He did not stop, singing out: "They tied a can to his tail . . ."

And the answer came: "De way to cook de possum sound . . ."

Then a rough-looking, sun-burned wreck of a man staggered in just to MacKinnon's left, and another tripped and dropped to MacKinnon's right.

The one on the ground looked up, blinked, and rolled over, hollering at his friend to MacKinnon's left who just kept going. MacKinnon spun around, fell to his knees, feeling his ribs give slightly. He pushed back up and reached out to grab the collar of the coat of a man who had almost walked right past him.

The stranger seemed startled as he mumbled: "Who are . . . ?" The wind and the sand forced him to turn around.

MacKinnon did not let go of the stranger's arm. He lowered his head, but not before two other men stepped out of the cloud of sand and dust.

Dust covered the bearded and grimy faces of the two men. He couldn't recognize them, or even describe them, but he knew neither was part of the group that had ridden into Bonito City what seemed like a million years ago. They had canteens strapped over their shoulders, and both wore revolvers around their middle, but he saw no long guns on these two. Now that all four were here, he saw that only two men carried rifles.

"Latch on!" MacKinnon said. "Grab hold of the last man!" he told them, nodding into the fury. "Latch on. Hold tight. Don't let go!"

He started moving, but it felt as though he were trying to pull a heavy farm wagon with a full load up a mountain.

"I've got a wagon this way! Latch on! Hold tight!" He started for the covered wreck of a wagon.

At least, he hoped he had not lost his bearings, and he prayed that the wagon was indeed just ahead.

Ol' Claude Ketchum went to the privy that night on the J-Bar-77 when I was riding the grub line. It was just snowing lightly when he left. Three, four minutes later, the wind started roaring across the Plains of San Agustine, driving snow that looked like a solid sheet of ice. The foreman should have strung up ropes from the privy and barn to the bunkhouse, but nobody expected that blizzard. A hundred feet. That's all the distance that separated the two-seater from the bunkhouse. Ol' Claude never made it back. Couldn't send no one to go look for him, not in that blizzard. Some of the boys found him, I heard whilst drinking in that cantina *in the Upper Frisco Plaza. Found him froze solid, forty feet from the privy. Figured he'd come out, got disoriented, started walking the wrong way. Opposite way. Turned back, and paralleled the bunkhouse before he just couldn't go any farther.*

"That," MacKinnon said to himself, his head bent in the wind, "ain't happening to me."

He knew where he was going. He had seen the wagon and the livestock. All he had to do was barrel straight ahead. One hundred yards. He kept counting his steps, small steps. He would squeeze to make sure he still gripped one of the men's wrists.

No one spoke. At least, he could not hear anyone behind him. He counted three hundred, and poked the carbine in front of him, swinging it from side to side. The wind almost jerked that out of his hand, too.

Nothing. He tried to raise his head higher, but sand blasted it back down.

Swearing, he kept walking. Ten yards. Twenty.

Don't panic. Don't sweat. That's what killed Ol' Claude.

He moved to his left, and kept pressing his fingers against the man's wrist. He tried to tell himself that this was not a blizzard. They wouldn't freeze to death. If they could find something of a wind block, all they had to do was brace themselves behind it. These storms blew out quickly.

Most times.

The arm he held jerked backward, almost

bringing MacKinnon to the ground. Turning, he found himself staring into the hard, wide, frightened eyes of one of the four men from the desert. The man tried to speak, but the effort only got him a mouthful of sand.

MacKinnon said: "We're all right!" He spun around, lowered his head, coughed. He took a step, and stopped. Leaning into the wind, he listened.

"Nothing in my . . ."

Then the voice died. MacKinnon pressed forward. He thought he heard "Thy cross I . . ."

"Florrie?" he mouthed. He started to yell for her to keep singing, but saved his breath. The wind would have carried his shout away from the wagon. It had been a miracle that he had been able to hear whoever had been singing at him, but he did not even hear that until the man was close.

Helpless, look to Thee for grace . . .

That way. He had been about to make the mistake Ol' Claude Cooper had made, walked the wrong way. MacKinnon turned, pushed himself. He moved with dogged determination. The wind moaned. He thought he heard Honey's whicker. And suddenly, he felt the wind lessen. Maybe it was a formation of rocks, causing the break in the wind he desperately needed.

Suddenly he could make out the wagon, and this was no mirage. He shoved the barrel of the Winchester and felt it slam into the water barrel. Florrie's angelic voice welcomed him home.

Rock of ages, cleft for me . . .

CHAPTER TWENTY-FOUR

"Name's Nelson Bookbinder," the lawman said after they had all settled inside the back of the wagon. Nelson Bookbinder was not certain the old Studebaker would support them all, but at least they were out of that infernal storm. He tapped his badge. "County sheriff. Deputy U.S. marshal. Ne'er-do-well." He smiled.

The little boy said: "What's a ne'er- . . . a ne'er-?"

"A no-account," the cowhand who had rescued them said, and grinned at the boy. "Like me."

"You ain't no . . . ne'er- . . . ne're- . . ."

"He sure ain't," said Mort. "We'd be buried out yonder if not for him. We thank you, mister."

"This is Mort," Bookbinder told them, and introduced Nikita and Davis, too. Then he waited.

Their rescuer frowned. "I'm Sam MacKinnon," he said.

"MacKinnon," Nelson Bookbinder said, just testing the word.

MacKinnon said nothing, just looked across the darkening wagon at the lawman.

Bookbinder's head shook. "Name doesn't ring a bell."

MacKinnon shrugged. "I guess that could be

a compliment, coming from a lawman such as yourself."

"You know me?"

MacKinnon shook his head again. "Nope. But I heard you stumping in Tularosa one time."

Bookbinder brushed sand off his duds, and chuckled. "That's the bad part of this job. Giving speeches. Almost as bad as getting your horses stolen from under your noses." He glared at Davis and Mort.

"Is that what happened?" the pretty blonde asked. She straightened at Bookbinder's gaze, and stammered as she introduced herself and her sister Florrie and brother Gary.

Bookbinder tipped his hat. Sand poured off the brim. "Yeah. Some rogues robbed a saloon in Bonito City on Sunday morning." He gave a condensed version of what had happened since. He kept his eyes on this saddle tramp named Sam MacKinnon.

The wind moaned, sometimes whistled, and never stopped as the wagon rocked and creaked. Dust drifted in. Sam MacKinnon read some dime novel to the boy. It was not one of those dreadfuls about Bookbinder and Nikita, though. It was even worse.

Florrie sneezed. No one responded till Gary asked: "Ain't somebody gonna say, 'God bless you?' "

"God bless you, little lady," Sheriff Nelson Bookbinder said, but he kept his eyes trained on MacKinnon, who had stopped reading. He leaned against the opening at the front of the wagon, trying to block any of the dust that drifted in from that direction, although the wind blew from the north.

On MacKinnon's left huddled Florrie and Gary. Katie sat on the cowhand's right. Crowded in the back were Mort and Davis over on the west-facing side, the latter rubbing his blistered feet, his boots off—the man had no socks. Mort busied himself trying to comb the sand out of his greasy hair with his fingers. Bookbinder sat directly across from MacKinnon. On his left, squatted Nikita.

"You should've God-blessed Florrie, Mister MacKinnon," Gary said.

MacKinnon looked at the boy. "Yeah," he said at length. "I reckon you're right. God bless you, Florrie."

The boy smiled. He was about to say something else, but MacKinnon said: "Best keep quiet, Gary. Don't want to fill your stomach with dirt."

"But what about the story?"

"I've read that to you four times, seems like."

"It's a good one, though."

"Later," MacKinnon said.

They passed the rest of the night in silence, and when the wind finally died, none spoke, a few snored. MacKinnon tossed fitfully, speaking in his sleep, and woke up just before dawn with those ribs tormenting him.

Katie retied the wrappings over MacKinnon's ribs that morning, while the Apache made coffee—Gary could not take his eyes off the Mescalero. Nelson Bookbinder walked around the camp, or what passed for a camp, and rubbed the neck of the blind mule and then the sorrel mare.

"Nice horse," Bookbinder said as he walked back to the fire.

"Not always," MacKinnon said.

The lawman chuckled. "Yeah, like most horses. People, too. You ever been to Bonito City, MacKinnon?"

He was direct. Sam MacKinnon had to give him that.

"Yeah," he answered. "A time or two."

"Recently?"

MacKinnon shook his head. "Can't say I'd call it recent."

MacKinnon looked at the horse. "I was in Bonito City. . . ." He paused to think. "I struck a notion to become a miner . . . didn't last but about two weeks . . . when the strike was made." He looked at the sky. " 'Eighty-two I guess. But I didn't own Honey back then."

All of that was true.

"I was thinking more recent," commented Bookbinder.

"Well, I got that mare about eighteen months ago."

"I'm thinking a few days ago. Sunday morning to be specific."

"He's been with us for two weeks!" Katie sang out. She had come back from the wagon with a battered old hat. "Oh. . . ." She put her hand on his side, gently. "I'm sorry. I didn't . . ."

But Florrie was looking up and saying: "Two weeks . . . why, Katie . . ."

"It's been two weeks, Florrie!" she snapped, and stood, glaring at her sister. "Two weeks." She turned to Bookbinder. "He rode upon us two weeks ago, Sheriff." She swallowed. "Our mother had died. He helped bury her." She started to point, but stopped. "He's been with us since. He buried her . . ."

"I helped," Gary chimed in.

"That's right. We all helped," Katie said. "But we never would have been able to . . . to do . . . to get . . . we'd likely be dead with Ma if he hadn't come along. Two weeks ago."

Bookbinder stared. Katie turned around, and told MacKinnon to stay where he was, but the cowhand was rising.

"What happened to your ribs?" the lawman asked.

235

He shrugged. "Busted them. Or something. They hurt like he- . . . well, they hurt."

"Horse throw you?"

MacKinnon nodded.

"Been dusted a time or two myself," Bookbinder said. "You helped bury their mother with busted ribs?"

"They helped."

"We all helped," Gary sang out, still looking at the Mescalero and the coffee pot.

"Sorry for your loss, folks," Bookbinder said, but he only glanced at Katie and Florrie before he stared through Sam MacKinnon. "You been helping them all this time? Two whole weeks?"

MacKinnon pointed at his side. "They've helped me quite a bit, too, Sheriff."

"He didn't have to help us," Katie said. "He could've kept riding."

The lawman's head bobbed. "Yeah. He could've kept riding yesterday, too. Didn't have to stop to help us." He wiped his jaw. "Ain't that coffee cooked yet, Nikita?"

A wagon came by, driven by a pudgy middle-aged man, with a woman in a pink and white checked dress, two younger men in bowlers and sack suits, and a woman rocking in a chair in the back with a spit can in her left hand as she dipped snuff. The driver stopped, chatted with

Bookbinder for a few minutes, before continuing the journey to Roswell.

Mort and Davis complained that they should have been allowed to ride with them to Roswell, especially seeing how Davis's feet were blistered and raw, and that Mort has been practically blinded by that dust storm.

"Where could you have fit on that wagon?" Florrie had asked.

"On the two mules," Mort replied.

Later, a stagecoach stopped. Bookbinder's badge acted like a closed gate. The Concord was packed with people, even some in the luggage boot on the back, and the top was crammed with two men and three boys, maybe twice the age of Gary. The stage left, too, moving fast to Roswell.

Mort and Davis wanted to take the stage, but the driver said if they could find room, and four dollars, they could ride. The two men sulked away to find a spot in the shade.

"You didn't want to go?" Katie asked.

Bookbinder shrugged, then nodded toward MacKinnon, who was tightening the bindings on the busted spokes. "If he can stay to help, after all he did for us . . . and you and your siblings . . . then I reckon we can stay, too." He studied MacKinnon for another moment, and made his way toward Katie. "Miss . . ."

She sang out in a nervous voice. "The desert's beautiful today, isn't it?" He had no time to answer. "Funny. Just how a storm like that can . . . I don't know, clear the air. Make things fresh. New." Her head nodded. "Yes. It's beautiful."

"If you say so, I reckon," Bookbinder said.

"What do you know about him, Miss Callahan?" he asked.

Her eyes widened. "What?"

"You heard me."

"I know enough."

"Where's your father?"

Her face hardened. "My father's dead."

"And your mother died of . . . ?"

"Consumption."

He nodded. "It sounds like I'm prying, miss, but . . ." He tapped his badge. "Part of the job. Records. Paperwork. And he . . . I mean, MacKinnon and you, and your brother and sister, you buried her."

"We had to," she said. "The wagon was busted. My . . . well, we lost one mule. Nobody stopped. Nobody cared. Till he showed up."

"And he stayed out of the goodness of his heart?"

"He stayed." Her eyes made him apologize. He had not realized how his question might have been misinterpreted.

"Two weeks, though. Even with that horse and that mule, you could have covered a lot of territory in two weeks." Bookbinder pulled on an ear lobe. "If you came through Ruidoso or even Tularosa, you could have gotten that wagon repaired. They've got real good wheelwrights in those towns. And being orphans, you could have . . ."

"My mother was strong-willed," Katie Callahan said. "She didn't believe in charity. I don't either. And maybe we didn't come through Ruidoso or Tularosa. Maybe we came from . . ."—she stopped to think—"Mesilla."

"Maybe. But you'd have had to come through Tularosa and Ruidoso if you were on the trail from Mesilla."

"Maybe we got lost."

He laughed, shook his head, and said: "So your mother, she died . . . whereabouts?"

Katie looked to the west. She pointed. "About a two-week ride from here," she said. "On a dilapidated wagon pulled by a blind mule and a saddle pony."

She walked away.

Bookbinder watched her go. He sighed and whispered: "Yeah, I reckon you did inherit that 'strong-willed' spirit from your ma, young lady."

CHAPTER TWENTY-FIVE

Bookbinder decided to try MacKinnon again when the cowboy, who the lawman thought was a saloon robber, was feeding the horses. The two younger kids were scrubbing the dishes—not that there had been much to eat—while the oldest had walked to the edge of the camp, admiring the sunset.

"Want a hand?" the lawman asked.

"I can handle it, but thanks."

"Nice horse."

"You've said that before."

"Well, you know how things get when you reach a certain age. Anyway, I was in Bonito City on Sunday morning and . . ."

"So I heard."

Bookbinder shook his head. "And I heard you've been with this family for two weeks." He figured he could test the cowhand now, and he turned from the horse, mule, and cowboy and found Katie Callahan. "She is a pretty girl."

"Watch where you're going, Sheriff. I've been in jail before. And you wouldn't be the first lawman I've throttled."

Turning back to MacKinnon, Bookbinder pushed back his hat. "I wasn't going anywhere, son. Just observing. Comes second nature after all these years I've lawed."

MacKinnon stepped toward him, and handed him the bucket of grain. "You want to observe something, Bookbinder, observe the horses." He shoved the bucket into the lawman's hand. "I'll take your offer of a hand, Bookbinder. Finish feeding Bartholomew and Honey."

He strode to the girl.

Sam MacKinnon reached for his hat when Katie turned around, and that made her giggle. He wore no hat. The wind had probably blown what he called a hat halfway to the Mexican border.

"Sam." She smiled.

"Umm." He pushed back his hair. "Katie."

The silence came. She hoped it wouldn't, but she knew it would. Now here it was. She saw the pain in his face, his eyes, and she knew it did not come from his ribs.

"You ought to know . . ."

"I know enough," she said, stopping him. "I know I'm not as good of a liar as you are, so don't tell me anything, Sam. Because I don't think I can get anything past that hard rock over yonder."

The stillness returned.

"Tonight," she whispered. "If a couple of fools could steal four horses from underneath their noses, then you could . . ."

"They weren't fools, Katie." His eyes held

on hers. "Well, at least two of them know what they're doing. Two of the four."

She had to look at the ground. "Sam . . ." Her head shook. "Sam . . ." When she looked at him again, she said: "You can still get away. Mexico. Texas."

"No."

He could be just as stubborn as she was. "Why not?"

He answered by staring at her. Katie started toward him, but stopped. "They're watching."

"We'll be in Roswell tomorrow," he told her. He drew in a deep breath, and let it out while shaking his head. "Could've made it in this evening if we'd pushed the animals, and us, some."

A heavy sigh followed another deep breath. "You figured out where you might be heading from Roswell?"

Her head shook. "You?"

He let out a mirthless chuckle. "I got a strong suspicion. There's a new prison opening up for business in Santa Fe shortly."

She walked to him, stopped at his side, and took his hand into hers. He had long fingers. He probably could play the piano, if he had the inclination to learn. They were tough, hard, and she tried to squeeze his hand.

"Katie, I got nothing to offer anybody," he said. "At best, I'm a thirty-a-month cowhand."

Her head nodded at the wagon. "You've seen my dowry, Sam."

He did not pull his hand away, and after a moment, he tightened his fingers around her small hand.

"But I'm older than . . ."

"Good Sam MacKinnon." She cut him off again. "Let's just see how things play out. All right? I've got a kid sister and a kid brother. No money. No home. I'm no catch."

"Well, I'm . . . it just don't make any sense for . . ."

"I'm glad you stayed," she told him.

Their hands relaxed, fell away, and MacKinnon again brushed his hair aside. "I am, too," he said.

"Why didn't you take that stagecoach to Roswell?" Nikita asked that night.

Bookbinder sipped his coffee. "I'm fishing."

"I don't like fish."

"You never ate my pa's catfish stew."

"I wouldn't want to."

"The men who left us to die in the desert . . . ," the Apache started, but Nelson Bookbinder silenced him.

"Are in Texas or Mexico by now." He nodded at MacKinnon. "But he knows their names. He's the one . . ."

Nikita finished the sentence for him. "That those two lazy dogs said they shot and killed in the mountains. I know. He's the one they left behind. With busted ribs."

"You figured that out yourself, did you?" Bookbinder said.

"I remember the horse from Bonito City."

"Like MacKinnon told us, there's a lot of sorrel horses in this part of the country."

"Not ridden by a man shooting at you."

Bookbinder rose, his knee joints popping. "The thing is, Nikita, he didn't shoot at us."

The Apache shrugged. "Hard rock that you are, I figured you'd have already arrested him by now."

The old lawman snorted. "In front of those kids. I'd never get re-elected."

"So we ride with them to Roswell?"

Bookbinder nodded. "Be there tomorrow. Maybe in time for that baseball stump match if we get an early enough start and the wagon don't fall apart and the horses don't go lame. I'm giving MacKinnon time to think about all he has done. See if he'll come to his senses and tell me the names of the men who rode into Bonito City with him. Judge'll go easier on him that way. I'd put in a word for him myself."

"And if he doesn't?"

"Then I lock him up in what passes for a jail in Roswell. Till he sings the tune I want to hear."

"Like the tune he was singing that brought us out of that sandstorm?" Nikita rose, too, stared hard at the lawman, and nodded at the badge. "That thing's light as a feather on you, Bookbinder. Most folks, they'd think it felt like an anchor." The Mescalero walked toward the wagon.

Bookbinder spit in the fire. "Educating Apaches ought to be a crime in this territory," he said to himself, and sat down to fill a cup with coffee.

CHAPTER TWENTY-SIX

Winds had blown down much of the red, white, and blue bunting, which no one had bothered to pick up, but the banner that stretched across the main street from the livery stable to the feed store greeted the wretched little wagon proudly, popping in the brisk wind.

ENGLE VERSUS ROSWELL—
ANNUAL STUMP MATCH
2 p.m. SATURDAY, JULY 25
25¢ Children, 50¢ Adults,
5¢ Draught Beers, Free Lemonade
Simon Hibler Town Field

Flicking the lines, Nelson Bookbinder shook his head, spit tobacco juice over the wagon's side, and muttered: "That's two things that make not one lick of sense to me."

MacKinnon lifted his head, yawned, and read the sign, but said nothing. He was just waking up. He was stuck sitting between the lawman and the Mescalero.

"Why," Bookbinder said, "would you name a field or park after a fellow that's still living? Fool could up and rob a bank, spit on the church floor, burn the whole town down. And why does anybody think hitting a puny ball with a fat stick is worth half a dollar to go watch."

Nikita said: "I saw the Engle boys play the bluecoats at the fort. Pretty good at it."

Bookbinder glowered at the Apache.

"They do this every year," MacKinnon said, as he started to drift back to sleep.

"What?" Bookbinder asked. "Play a stump match?"

MacKinnon lifted his head again. "Yeah."

"You play that fool game?" Bookbinder asked.

MacKinnon shook his head. "Kid I punched cattle with for the Bar Cross did, though. Pretty good at it. Good ballist. That's what they call them. Good cowboy, too, when he didn't have his nose buried in some book."

That boy read Homer and Shakespeare and just about any book he could get his hands on. Me? I've read maybe twenty penny dreadfuls in my whole life. He grinned as he thought about the young cowboy. *Read the same dime novel maybe six times in the past few days.*

The streets of Roswell were deserted, but far beyond the hodge-podge of town buildings, flags popped in the wind, unsaddled horses pranced in two big corrals, and buggies, farm wagons, and covered wagons sat parked in the sand. The wind blew toward the east, carrying the sounds of shouts, cheers, and jovial banter.

"Must be two o'clock," the lawman said as he looked up to find the sun.

The sign on Bransford's Livery said **Closed**. The sign on the feed store said **Closed**. The shades were drawn at the post office. The sign tacked to the door at the bank read: **CLOSED FOR TOWN HOLIDAY**. When Bookbinder stopped the wagon at one adobe, Nikita leaped out and tried the door to the Doctor/Barber/Undertaker. The door did not budge. He knocked, turned back, and gave MacKinnon and Bookbinder a shrug.

"I reckon Pres Lewis is at that game, too," Bookbinder said, shaking his head. He spit tobacco juice into the street, leaned toward the door next to the town marshal's office, and yelled: "Maginnis? You there?"

Nikita tried that door, as well. It was open, he went in, then came back out, shaking his head.

"Davis! Mort!" Bookbinder called to his men in the back.

"Yes, sir?" one of them mumbled.

"Get off your behinds and run over to that ball field. Find the sheriff, Maginnis. Find the doctor, Pres Lewis. Fetch them back here. *Pronto*, boys."

The two men slipped off what was left of the tailgate, and let their bowed legs carry them to the eastern edge of Roswell.

The Holland House stood across the street, and someone moved behind the curtains in the dining

248

room, so Bookbinder clucked his tongue, and turned the wagon across the street. This time he stopped the wagon, set the brake, and climbed out of the Studebaker. MacKinnon had fallen back asleep.

Down the street, horses were tethered to the hitching rail in front of the Río Hondo Saloon. He looked that way, considered going inside, but decided against it. "Miss Callahan," he called out, and Katie stepped out of the rear of the wagon.

"Let's see if we can get you fixed up," Bookbinder said, indicating the hotel, The Holland House, with a nod of his head. "Your brother and sister still asleep?"

"Yes, sir."

"Let them sleep. But maybe we can get the three of you a bed."

"And a bath?" she asked.

Bookbinder smiled warmly. "Yes, ma'am."

After helping her down, Bookbinder turned to see two men coming out of the hotel. They stopped immediately. The young one straightened. The older man squinted hard, sniffled, and let his mouth fall open.

" 'Afternoon," Bookbinder said.

"Yes," the younger one said. He blinked, and seemed to take in Bookbinder for the first time. Bookbinder did not look away from the two. He could tell they were staring at either Nikita or MacKinnon up in the wagon. The older man was squinting hard, and had his right hand on the butt of a holstered revolver.

Bookbinder didn't think the two were looking at the Apache.

"Got too much sun, I see," Bookbinder said.

"Yeah. I mean, yes, sir." The young man's hat looked to be fresh off the shelf of the mercantile. He wet his lips.

Bookbinder removed his own hat. "We did, too. Had a long walk." He waved his hat toward the east. "Through that."

"Well," the boy said. He saw Katie, and tipped his new hat. "Ma'am." With his hat off, he acknowledged Bookbinder. "Sheriff."

"Not sheriff, son," the lawman responded. "Not today. I've got no authority as a sheriff in Roswell. But as a deputy federal marshal, I do. Shooting at a federal lawman's a crime, too."

"Yes, sir." The younger grabbed the older man's shoulder. "Come on, Sherm. We best be getting back to . . . the um . . . ranch."

"Huh?" But the squinting man offered no resistance as the kid pulled him away from the hotel and down the street.

"Do you know those men, Mister Bookbinder?" Katie asked.

"Not by name, miss," the lawman answered, and looked up at MacKinnon, whose head bobbed as he dozed in the seat. Bookbinder made no move to enter The Holland House.

The two men made a beeline for the Río Hondo Saloon. A wiry Mexican came up from the alley—from one of the cribs, Bookbinder figured—and started toward the same watering hole when the young man called out: "Chico!"

The Mexican had his hands on the saloon's batwing doors, but he stopped, frowned, and waited for the two to reach him.

Bookbinder could not hear what was said as the three stood outside the saloon, but he saw the Mexican straighten and look past the two. He was still staring, just standing in front of the saloon's entrance, when the other two moved to the hitching rail. Both pulled around their horses, and hurried into the saddles, spurring the horses down the road as soon as they were seated.

They did not stop at Simon Hibler Town Field.

"Those weren't our horses," Nikita said.

"No," confirmed the lawman, as he watched the Mexican push through the batwing doors.

"Why would they still be in town?" Nikita asked.

"I don't know," Bookbinder said. "But go to the livery. I don't care how you get in, but get in. Check the corral there, too. If you find our horses, get back to me and I mean immediately. MacKinnon!" He stepped to the wagon, reached up, and punched the cowhand's thigh.

MacKinnon's head jerked up.

"Is anything the matter, Mister Bookbinder?" Katie asked.

"Not sure, miss," he said, but he did not look at her.

MacKinnon shook the sleep out of his brain, and looked down at the lawman.

After pulling a few greenbacks from his pocket, Bookbinder held them up to MacKinnon. "Get a room for us. And a room for Miss Katie and the children. Get them a bath. I'll be back directly."

MacKinnon remained on the wagon seat, sniffing, still half asleep, watching the lawman as he made his way toward the Río Hondo Saloon.

He studied the money in his hand, looked to his right and down at Katie, who appeared as confused as he did. "Where's the Apache?" he asked her.

"Mister Bookbinder sent him to the livery, even though it's closed."

"What for?"

She shrugged.

Chico Archuleta found Jace Martin sitting at a corner table, alone, dealing solitaire. A large stein of beer sat at Martin's left. Glancing at the pocket watch beside the deck, Martin said: "Where are the others? It's time to see how that baseball . . ."

"Bookbinder's outside," Archuleta said.

Martin's cold eyes deadened. "That can't be."

"It can be. And Four-Eyes and the kid just lit a shuck."

Martin laid the deck on the table. "The Apache?"

"He's with him."

With a curse, Martin balled both hands into fists.

"We've got to ride hard, boss," Archuleta said.

"With all that money at the ticket gate?" he asked.

"We've got all that money from Charley The Trey's place," Archuleta reminded him.

"But I want more."

"You can have my share," Archuleta said. "Because I can't spend it if I'm dead. Or in prison."

He turned and hurried toward the batwing doors.

"Howdy, Chico."

Nelson Bookbinder smiled, but his right hand remained on the butt of his holstered revolver.

Archuleta swung around, his hand dropping— then freezing—at his own revolver as he backed into the wooden post that held up the saloon's awning.

"I didn't recognize you back in Bonito City, Chico. How you been?"

"*Yo no sabe*," Archuleta said.

Chuckling, Bookbinder shook his head. "Chico,

you speak English better than three-quarters of the white folks in this territory. Why don't we take a stroll down to Maginnis's office? I'm interested in seeing if my horse is in the livery stable here. I know Bransford never did pay much attention to bills of sale, but he always recollects who traded him a horse." He nodded toward the marshal's office.

"*Yo no sabe*," Archuleta repeated.

"You could make things easier on me, Chico, if you'd tell me the names of those two fellows who just left town at a high lope. And anyone else who was with you in Bonito City. Help yourself out, too. I can put in a word to a judge."

"*Yo no sabe*."

Bookbinder sighed. "If that's the way you want to play this hand . . ." The revolver came out quickly, and Bookbinder's thumb cocked the hammer as he shoved the barrel just below Archuleta's rib cage, causing Archuleta to grimace as he was forced back against the hitching rail. The horses at the hitch rail began prancing nervously, pulling the reins and ropes tight.

Bookbinder brought the revolver up, still cocked, but now aimed at Archuleta's face. He never moved the pistol as his left hand reached for the handcuffs that dangled from the shell belt on his left side.

The Adam's apple of the Mexican bobbed. He held his breath.

"Turn around, Chico," Bookbinder said, and then he tensed as the batwing doors behind him squeaked.

He started turning when Jace Martin rammed the barrel of his revolver against the side of the lawman's skull. Bookbinder's gun roared, causing Chico Archuleta to scream in pain as he clutched his ear, blackened and burned by the muzzle flash. Archuleta fell over the rail as Jace Martin swore.

The horses at the hitch rack began pulling away from the rail, tearing free from ropes, hackamores, and reins. Two of the horses bolted east. A third reared and whinnied. Archuleta came up in an instant, lunged, grabbed the halter of a buckskin. The gelding dragged him a couple of feet, but the *vaquero* was good.

Jace Martin stepped over the unconscious form of Nelson Bookbinder, in an attempt to reach the remaining dun. Archuleta was already jumping into the saddle without even using the stirrups. Leaning low, he swore as the buckskin carried him west, toward the ball park, toward Texas.

Swearing, Jace Martin watched his partner escape. Even worse, the big dun galloped after Chico Archuleta.

Martin swung toward the saloon, snapped a shot off that busted two slats from the swinging batwing doors.

"Stay inside!" he barked. "Show your face, I'll blow it off."

He kept the smoking barrel aimed at the saloon as he ducked to pick up Bookbinder's revolver off the hard-packed dirt.

When he looked back down the street, he saw a dark-skinned man in a black hat running from the livery. Nikita! Martin raised his pistol and fired a shot, seeing the dust fly up yards ahead of the Apache. It made the scout stop, however, because he wasn't armed. He had been running toward the wagon parked in front of The Holland House.

That's when Martin saw the man in the driver's box, pushing himself to a standing position. The man wore no hat. The sun was high. But Jace Martin could make out Sam MacKinnon's face clearly.

Martin's lips mouthed a silent curse, and he whispered: "No . . ."

He swung around, guns in both hands, and ran toward the baseball game being played at Simon Hibler Town Field. He could find a horse there, ride hard and fast for Texas, or even Mexico. Get away from Nelson Bookbinder, and as far away from that sharp Mescalero Apache scout.

Get away from MacKinnon.

CHAPTER TWENTY-SEVEN

"Oh my," Katie Callahan said. Her hands were covering her mouth, but then she grabbed the hems of her ragged skirt, and ran toward Nelson Bookbinder, lying in front of the Río Hondo Saloon.

Sam MacKinnon clutched his right side, as gently as he could, as he moved to the inside of the wagon. Florrie and Gary were watching their sister run through the opening in the back of the wagon.

"What's happening?" Florrie asked.

"Hey, kids." The boy and girl turned and stared at MacKinnon. "Help me down. Be quick."

Jace Martin slowed down, holstered his revolver, and shoved Bookbinder's into the waistband at his back. He removed his hat, wiped his forehead, and tried to smile as he approached McEwen's Mercantile. A man in an apron and sleeve garters stepped outside, and stared past Martin, looking up and down the street.

"What's all that shooting?" the merchant asked.

Martin hooked his thumb behind him, but did not slow his gait. "Drunks." He laughed. "Celebrating the ball game, I guess. Scared off their horses. Idiots."

The man seemed to scrutinize Martin, who nodded and simply kept right on walking.

Nikita reached Bookbinder first. He slowly rolled the lawman over, frowned at the blood matting his hair and staining his collar, but let out a breath of relief when he saw that the lawman's chest was still rising and falling. Then Katie Callahan was at his side, dropping to her knees. She looked up and saw men standing in the saloon's doorway, keeping the batwing doors in front of them as some sort of protection.

"I need a towel. Clean if you have one," she said to them. "And whiskey."

The men blinked.

"And I need it right now," she said, lips tight, the words carefully spaced and the tone unmistakable. The men scattered like quail.

Nikita stood up, planning to go after Jace Martin, but Katie stopped him.

"Nikita, find that doctor. Find him now."

Frowning, the Mescalero pointed at Martin who was about to disappear behind the Saragosa House.

"Now, Nikita. His skull might be fractured," she told him. "That man buffaloed him hard with his pistol."

The Apache stared at her and at the unconscious lawman, then nodded. He moved down the street, thinking the doctor would most likely be at the stump match, anyway.

A young cowboy with red hair and an older one missing the top joints of three fingers on his left hand, plowed out through the batwing doors. One handed Katie a towel. It was wet with beer, but at least it wasn't that dirty. The other one pulled the cork out of a bottle of rye. He shoved it right under her face.

"Miss," he said, and tipped his hat.

She took the bottle, and, holding it away from Bookbinder, she soaked the wet rag with the whiskey. She was starting to bring it to the knot and the large cut on the side of the old lawman's head when she heard the sound of jingling spurs.

Katie's hands froze as Sam MacKinnon crossed the sandy alley, and moved past the two cowboys, Nelson Bookbinder, and Katie Callahan. He did not appear to notice anything.

"Oh, my God," Katie whispered.

A fat man in a checkered sack suit stepped out of the Saragosa House, and almost knocked Martin into the street. Martin reached up to keep his hat from sailing off, but was too late. He stopped his fall by catching the column post, slipped onto the street, cursing as the fat man blubbered some sort of apology. But Martin kept moving and made his way around the corner.

"Mister . . . hey, mister!" the fat man cried out. "Your hat, mister. You forgot your hat!"

Martin paid no mind to the man's calls as he

was hit by the smell of roasting peanuts and smoke. His eyes took in Dutch ovens sitting over open fires, lined up buggies, and two corrals full of horses. But the corrals were surrounded by cowboys itching for a fight fueled by beer and all the excitement, and guns hung on the hips of practically every one of those cowhands.

Martin swallowed. He had to think. He reached up, smoothed his hair, and moved down the side of a building, thinking he had come up with the answer. He would double back and head for the livery. The owner was here watching the baseball game between Engle and Roswell. Bransford had bragged about that when Martin had haggled with him over the trade of those horses—Marshal Bookbinder's horses. If he ran fast enough, he could bust into the livery, saddle a fast thorough-bred—the one Bransford had refused to trade. He'd be raising dust for Mexico this time, before MacKinnon or anyone else knew he was gone.

He turned the corner, only to find two of the deputies from Bookbinder's posse. They weren't even looking in Martin's direction, just sharing a bottle of whiskey with some Mexican, but all had guns. One of them looked up in Martin's direction.

Spinning around, Martin moved back toward the corrals, brought his hand to his head, and cursed again. A cracking sound came from the field where the two teams were starting to play ball, and the men, women, and children began to cheer and wave their little flags.

Martin lowered his head. He saw the people sit back down on the bleachers, and he blinked, amazed at just how many people had turned out for this event.

Smiling, Martin moved toward the entryway. He'd hide out in the crowd till he could safely get away. And if someone did come in and find him, well, he had two revolvers, since he took that law dog's.

"Fifty cents."

The cracking voice stopped him. Martin looked up, glaring at some pock-marked teenager holding out a grubby little hand.

"Fifty cents," the kid repeated.

"What?"

"It costs fifty cents to see the ball game, mister. Unless you're a kid. Then it's only two bits. But you don't look like a kid."

"Hasn't the game already started?" Martin tried.

"Sure. Just started. Our boys are batting first. You still got to pay. And it's for civic improvement, you see. A good cause. Those boys playing aren't professionals. They're just playing for fun, you see. The money goes to . . ."

Martin became flustered. There, before him, was the cashbox. And at the table to his right, men were taking bets, writing in ledgers, and putting money in another box.

It would've been so beautiful, he thought, *but at least I have all of the money from Charley The Trey's place. No, I don't. Most of that is in the saddlebags on that dun chasing after Chico Archuleta.*

Swearing, he reached inside his vest pocket, only to find gold pieces. The boy ticket-taker smiled patiently. Martin shoved his hand into his pants pocket and brought out a nickel. He handed that to the boy.

"Well," the boy said. "That's a start."

Glancing over his shoulder, Martin frowned. He saw Sam MacKinnon had stepped off the dirt and gravel path that ended at the Saragosa House. Martin swore, but at least MacKinnon was staring at the corrals. Martin's hand returned to his vest pocket, and he pulled out a double-eagle. He slammed it into the boy's hand.

"Well," the boy stammered. "I don't know if I can make change."

Martin pushed past him. "It's for Roswell's civic improvement," he said.

"But you need your ticket, mister."

He kept walking, head bent, moving to the fellow in a white cap who kept yelling: "Peanuts. Roasted nuts. Get your roasted nuts, ladies and gents."

"Hey!" The boy at the ticket gate just would not shut up. "You can't . . ."

• • •

"You can't come in here wearing no guns, mister!"

MacKinnon was making a beeline for the corrals when the shout from near the ball field caused him to pivot. A kid, wearing a pillbox cap of black wool with yellow horizontal stripes across the top above the brim, stood waving a small piece of paper in his right hand.

MacKinnon spotted Jace Martin, no hat but a gun belt on his hip, brush past another fellow at a peanut stand, and disappear in the shadows of the bleachers.

Sam MacKinnon made his way toward the ticket gate.

Shaking his head, the boy turned around and shoved the ticket into his pocket and tossed the gold coin into the money box. He wet his lips and started to smile as MacKinnon walked toward the field. His mouth opened, but no words came out as he watched the hard-scrabbled man, holding his left hand over his right side, walk straight through the gate and toward the playing field. Something told the kid to keep his trap closed.

Jace Martin pushed. He saw the ballplayers, dressed in ridiculous outfits out in the field. Some sat and others stood behind the benches.

"That pitch was a strike!" yelled a man in a black hat and suit.

Martin's eyes looked to the man yelling. A star was pinned to the lapel of his vest.

"Are you blind, Marshal?" someone in the crowd yelled. "That wasn't nowhere near home plate!"

Martin moved down, looking for a seat, but the people were on their feet at the moment, so he couldn't tell if there was any space open. There had to be more people here than lived in Roswell. The barkeep hadn't been kidding. Martin moved to the side, and then he saw horses way off, several yards behind the man in the straw hat and bib-front shirt standing well beyond the man throwing the balls. People too cheap or unable to afford the fifty-cent ticket were watching the game from way back yonder.

Martin moved to the edge of the fence. It was a long walk to get to the horses. He glanced at the marshal umpiring the game. The lawman did not wear a gun.

"Hey, mister, no guns allowed at this here game!" a big, beefy man yelled at Martin, and moved toward him. "Hey, you hear me?"

Jace Martin didn't have much of a choice. He stepped onto the field and made a beeline for those horses.

"What the Sam Hill!" The man who was moving his arm like a windmill, stopped, and dropped the baseball. The man holding the bat-stick stepped aside, cursed, and sprayed tobacco juice into the dirt.

The marshal stepped in front of the pitcher, grabbed his vest, and flaunted his badge, saying: "Get off the playing field, you damned fool!"

Hesitating, Martin stopped, trying to figure out what to do. The crowd in the stands began booing and hissing. A hurled sarsaparilla bottle just missed his head. The man with the bat-stick started toward Martin, so he turned, and moved back—only to come to a stop. He cursed.

Sam MacKinnon was stepping out onto the field now.

"Hey!" the marshal yelled to Martin's back. "That's a gun in your waistband."

"There's one in his holster, too!" the pitcher advised the lawman.

Someone screamed. MacKinnon continued to walk toward Martin.

So Jace Martin pulled the gun from his holster and thumbed back the hammer.

"Boys!" someone yelled from one of the ballists' benches. "That's Sam MacKinnon."

Martin squeezed the trigger, just clipping MacKinnon's hair, but that didn't stop him and the fool kept right on coming.

"I'll kill you!" Martin warned MacKinnon as he turned and snapped off another shot that caused the marshal and the pitcher to drop onto their bellies. The ball rolled to the first baseman, one of the cowboys from Engle.

By that time, there was quite a commotion among the people watching the game. The women were gathering up the children and heading out of the park. A few screamed, and a number of children began to cry.

Jace Martin turned around, cocking the revolver.

"MacKinnon!" he yelled. He was pulling the trigger when the baseball busted his ear.

A gun roared, and MacKinnon felt another slug whistle past his head. He did not stop. He did not even consider doing such a thing.

"You need a hand, Sam?"

MacKinnon shot a glance at the young man who had thrown the baseball. It was that crazy teenager from the Bar Cross, the one always looking for a horse to break, a book to read, a ball game to play, or someone to fight.

"It's me, Sam. Gene! Gene Rhodes."

MacKinnon didn't take time to respond. Shaking clarity back into his head, Jace Martin had scrambled to his knees. He looked at the ball in the dirt, then at the pistol beyond his reach. MacKinnon looked back just as Jace Martin started pulling the revolver from behind his back. The gun was cocked, but by then MacKinnon was close and he kicked Martin in the groin.

The breath shot out of MacKinnon's lungs, and he doubled over from the misery in his ribs, dropping to his knees. He spit, and found Martin, on his knees, too, his left hand clutching his privates, right hand still holding the revolver, drool spilling from his mouth.

Martin brought the weapon up, saying: "You son-of- . . ." And MacKinnon powered his right fist into the side of Martin's jaw.

Collapsing to the ground, MacKinnon felt something wet leak from his own mouth. Blood? He wasn't sure.

"Fight!" one of the Roswell ballists shouted.

"Get him!" another yelled.

MacKinnon tried to breathe. He had done some stupid things in his life, but coming, unarmed, after a man armed with two six-shooters, well, that might have been the dumbest. His chest heaved, his insides screamed, but he pushed himself up in an attempt to stand.

Martin slammed the barrel of the pistol into MacKinnon's unprotected side. Down went MacKinnon.

"Should we help him?" someone yelled.

"Ain't my fight," a cowhand answered.

The marshal had risen. "You pull that trigger, mister," he said, "and you'll swing for murder."

Martin turned, aimed the gun at the marshal and the crowd, and then brought the weapon around at MacKinnon again.

But now MacKinnon had the bat-stick in his left hand. And he swung it like a reaper, catching Martin between the ankles and his knees. The gun fired. The bullet plowed up part of the first-base line, and Martin lay writhing on the ground.

"Help him! For the love of God, help him!"

Dully, MacKinnon recognized Katie Callahan's voice.

"Sam!" she cried. "Oh, God, help him!"

Martin pushed himself to a seated position. He tried to cock the revolver. But fueled by anger, MacKinnon stood up, still holding the bat-stick in his left hand. Bringing the heavy piece of wood level with his waist, MacKinnon grabbed the big end of the piece of wood with his right hand, and dived as Martin leveled the pistol. The bat-stick caught Martin high on his chest, drove him to the ground, and rolled up onto his throat. Feeling insatiable rage, MacKinnon pressed harder on the piece of ash, and closed his eyes from pain, or maybe just hatred.

"Sam!" Katie kept calling. "Sam! Sam! Please, Sam . . . don't!"

His eyes opened. He saw the bat on Martin's throat, how pale the man looked, the fear in his eyes, heard that wastrel sucking for air that he could not find.

Releasing his grip on the bat-stick, MacKinnon

rolled off. His chest heaved. His ribs hurt like they had never hurt before. Beside him, Jace Martin kept gagging.

Gene Rhodes's excited, boyish face appeared above MacKinnon. "That was some fight, boys." He started emptying the bullets from one of Martin's guns.

Katie touched MacKinnon's forehead. His eyes opened. She tried to smile as she wiped the tears from her face.

"Silly fool," she whispered, brought his right hand to her lips, kissed it, and squeezed his hand hard. "Silly . . . silly . . . silly."

Marshal Maginnis, the umpire, suddenly appeared by MacKinnon and Katie.

"Somebody better explain to me what the devil this was all about, and it had better be a real good story."

"I can do that, Maginnis."

Holding a dingy towel that reeked of stale beer and fresh whiskey against his bloodied head, Nelson Bookbinder stepped over Jace Martin.

"Nelson?" the town marshal said.

Bookbinder pointed at the smoking revolver that Gene Rhodes still held. "Mind handing me my pistol, sonny?"

Rhodes paled, but he quickly spun it around, butt forward, and let the lawman take it and slide it into his holster.

"You busted up a good ball game, Nelson," Marshal Maginnis said.

"Yeah. . . ." A hand with long fingers was reaching over and probing Bookbinder's bleeding head. "Get away from me, Doc," the lawman snapped at Pres Lewis. "Check out MacKinnon there. His ribs was banged up before he tangled with this reprobate."

Bookbinder stared down at Jace Martin.

"I've been on the trail of this rapscallion since he and some other boys robbed Charley The Trey's Three of Spades in Bonito City. Tracked them into that furnace between here and there." He shook his head, cringed at the pain, and spit tobacco juice between Martin's legs. "And his boys up and stole our horses. In the desert. Left us in that wasteland to suffer and die." The quid of tobacco moved to the opposite cheek. "That ain't nice."

"You let your horses get stole?" Maginnis said. "From under your nose?"

"Nikita did," Bookbinder replied.

"Bull," the Apache said, having just arrived on the field. But when everyone looked at him, he shrugged. "Well . . . maybe."

"Is this fellow your deputy, Nelson?" Maginnis asked.

The doctor was on his knees now, pulling up MacKinnon's shirt. Pres Lewis asked: "Did you bandage him, Nelse?"

"No." Bookbinder pointed. "She did."

"Well, who is he?" someone asked.

"He's a man to ride the river with," the teenage cowboy, Gene Rhodes, said. "Can't find nobody better. He taught me a lot two years back when I was just a tenderfoot."

Bookbinder nodded. "He's a man to ride the river with. That's plain enough. He come across this young lady here in that desert. Her ma had died. Her . . ." Bookbinder figured to leave out the part about the wastrel of a father. "Her pa was dead some time back. They lost a mule. Busted a wheel. Nobody would stop for them. Ain't that a terrible state of affairs. Some folks was in too big of a hurry to come to this baseball game, so they left a bunch of kids in that wasteland to die. But this fellow here, Sam MacKinnon, did something, stove up as he was. Helped bury their mother. Got them, and me and my deputies, through the worst sandstorm I've ever seen. Got us all here. Fools have written me up in nickel-priced books of lies, but they ought to write the truth about MacKinnon. He hauled me and Nikita and my two deputies, wherever they are right now . . . likely drunk . . . out of that furnace." Bookbinder looked down at Jace Martin. "And he caught the man who led that robbery of Charley The Trey's place."

Looking up at Bookbinder, Jace Martin cursed.

"MacKinnon was with me, Marshal. He helped rob Charley's place."

Katie Callahan sucked in a deep breath.

"Is that a fact?" Bookbinder asked.

"It is. It's a wonder you don't recognize him. Or his horse."

"Who else was with you?"

Martin shook his head. "I don't squeal on my pards."

"You just said MacKinnon was with you."

"It's different."

Bookbinder shrugged. "All right." He spit again. "How many men rode with you? You can tell me that, can't you?"

"Three others."

The lawman nodded. "Like the three curs that rode out of town when we came here, including the one who wanted to split my skull in front of the Río Hondo. That was Chico Archuleta. Five altogether. That right?"

"Yeah. But I don't know any Chico Archuleta."

Bookbinder looked at the crowd of ballists and spectators. "I happened to be in Bonito City on Sunday morning. That's how come Nikita and I went after them. Got a good jump on them, too. Five men robbed Charley's place. That's a fact. I got men with me. Mort! Davis!" He had to yell three more times before the two men came onto the field between the pitcher's line and the batsman's lines.

"Tell Jace Martin, Marshal Maginnis, and everyone here what happened in the mountains right after the robbery in Bonito City," Bookbinder said.

The two men stared at each other.

Bookbinder prodded. "Just like you told me."

"I . . . well . . . we . . . um . . . we killed one of those bandits," Mort said.

"One shot," Davis added. "Through . . ." He tapped his chest.

"There," Mort finished, and pointed.

"Where was his horse?" Bookbinder asked.

"Well . . . it must have . . ." Mort looked at Davis.

"Throwed him. Or . . ."

Mort finished for Davis. "They might have pushed him off. To make us, the posse, sort of . . ."

"Go after him," Davis said. "That's what we did."

"That's exactly what happened," Jace Martin said, beaming at testimony that would send him to the new penitentiary in Santa Fe. Coughing, he began to massage his throat.

"Let them talk," Bookbinder said, and nodded at his two deputies.

"But Marshal Bookbinder and him . . ."—Mort nodded at Nikita—"they rode on ahead. After . . ." He looked down at Martin.

Davis blinked. "After I shot the man in the mountains. The fella this *hombre* left behind."

"But I saw him first," Mort said.

"That's a bald-faced lie!" Jace Martin tried to get up, but Bookbinder shoved him to the ground.

"I said let them talk, buster," Bookbinder said. "If you think about it, and think long and hard, you'll know there's one mistake you don't want to make right about now. So you sit there, you study on things, and you let my two deputies finish. You'll get your say in court, if you live long enough."

Turning back to the two deputies, Bookbinder chose Davis. "Where was this bad *hombre* shot?"

"Right through his brisket." Again, Davis tapped his chest.

"And where is the body?"

They waited, silently, looking at each other, then at Jace Martin, then at the cowhand and the girl. Mort swallowed. Davis shuffled his feet.

"I'm waiting," Bookbinder said.

"We buried him," Mort said.

"Not really," Davis added. "See, he fell in a hole."

"Sinkhole," Mort said.

"Or a den for a fox," Davis said.

"Or some other wild animal."

"We kind of covered up the hole," Davis added.

"Might not be able to find it," Mort said. "It was getting dark, you see."

"And we wanted to catch up with the marshal."

"That's it?" Bookbinder asked.

Both men nodded sheepishly, as they looked down into the dirt.

Bookbinder nodded. "There you have it."

"That's a bunch of hogwash," Martin said. "MacKinnon was in on this job with us. You saw him. You all saw him."

Bookbinder stared at the two deputies. "Can you identify this man, boys? This Good Sam MacKinnon. Can you say he was one of the robbers at Bonito City?"

This time, the men shook their heads, and Mort said evenly: "Couldn't. They all had sacks over their heads."

"Wheat sacks," Davis said.

"That'll do, boys. I'm not sure we'll ever catch the other bandits, but that's all right. We've got this man. And he has already confessed to the robbery. Isn't that right, Maginnis?"

"I'll swear to it in court, Nelson. He wasn't even provoked."

"You're not getting away with this, Book-binder!" Martin shouted as he tried to stand up, but Bookbinder stepped on his shoulder and kept him down.

"You can't do that, law dog. I say MacKinnon was in on the robbery with me."

"My deputies say he wasn't. I don't question my deputies, boy. They're sworn to tell the truth."

"You're a liar!"

The gun came out of Bookbinder's holster, and

the lawman slowly pulled back the hammer.

"I've had you in my jail in Lincoln a few times, Jace Martin. I've had some crimes I would have liked to have arrested you for, too, only couldn't quite get enough for a judge or jury. You're a card cheat, a rustler, and I believe you've likely done worse. Murder, maybe. And I know you've robbed at least one saloon and gambling parlor in my jurisdiction. And there's one thing that a punk like you ought to learn, and you should have learned it a long, long time ago. You can get away with a lot of things, boy. Cheating at cards. Throwing a wide loop and slapping a running iron on beef that's not yours. You can bust up a game of baseball, disturb the peace, insult a young lady, and slam a gun into the head of a deputy United States marshal as he's making an arrest of a fellow suspected of committing a crime. But one thing you never do, boy, and that's call someone you don't know well a liar."

He pulled the trigger.

And laughed at the look on Jace Martin's face when the hammer snapped on an empty chamber.

Katie Callahan was breathing again, and her heart started to slow down. She kissed MacKinnon's hand before letting Bookbinder help her to her feet. The doctor continued to work on MacKinnon's chest.

"This baseball contest is postponed," Maginnis

said. "At least for the time being. I'm deputizing you Roswell boys to get this cur to the jail. You Engle boys, round up all the equipment and leave it at the feedstore. We'll figure out when we can resume this game."

"Fetch a wagon," Pres Lewis said without looking up. "Some blankets. Let's find a place to take this young man."

"Come on, Miss Callahan," Nelson Bookbinder said as he led her away. "We best find your brother and sister."

CHAPTER TWENTY-EIGHT

The door opened, and Sam MacKinnon watched Nelson Bookbinder, hat in hand, step inside the first-floor room at The Holland House. The lawman looked around, laid his hat, crown down, atop a dresser, and pulled up a chair beside the bed where MacKinnon lay.

"How you feel?" Bookbinder asked.

MacKinnon rolled his eyes.

"Well, it's your own fault. You should've left Jace Martin to me."

"How do you feel?" MacKinnon asked.

The lawman touched the white bandage that wrapped his head where Martin had tried to dent his head. With a grin, he rolled his eyes. "Nice of them to put you on the ground floor," Bookbinder said, just to fill the silence.

MacKinnon managed a shrug.

"Town chipped in," Bookbinder said. "Room's paid for. For you and the girl and her siblings. Doctor's paid for. A local rancher even bought Miss Katie a new wagon . . . John Wesley Pringle's outfit. I guess you rode for that brand, too, MacKinnon." Bookbinder looked at the floor, one way, then the other, and finally found the cuspidor. He dragged it closer, sent a stream of tobacco juice into it, and straightened. " 'Course, we had to tell her all of those things were bought from the reward you got for capturing Jace Martin."

MacKinnon's mouth cracked open.

"Miss Callahan won't take any charity, you know."

MacKinnon smiled.

"And here's something you might find interesting. Pres Lewis said he would donate a tombstone to Miss Katie's mother. Even bring the body back, plant her in the cemetery, but do you know what that girl said?" Bookbinder chuckled. "She said moving her ma to a graveyard might be proper, but the tombstone you carved, that's what she wanted over the grave. And her sister and her brother, they backed up that spunky girl." Bookbinder laughed again. "Girl. That's some woman."

The clock ticked on the dresser. Bookbinder shifted the chewing tobacco to his other cheek, and said: "No sign of Chico or those two other fellows who helped rob Charley The Trey's place in Bonito City."

"How about the fifth man?" MacKinnon asked, staring at the curtains in the window.

"Well, you heard what Mort and Davis said. That fellow's dead in some hole in the mountains."

MacKinnon nodded.

Bookbinder worked his tobacco. "And, yeah, I

heard what Jace Martin said." His head bobbed. "I expect, he'll say it again in court. Under oath."

"Yeah," MacKinnon said. He drew in a breath, let it out, and turned to look at the lawman. "Bookbinder, you know good and well . . ."

Nelson Bookbinder raised his right hand, fingers extended, to silence MacKinnon.

"MacKinnon, I am an officer of the court. Sworn to uphold the law, so you let me speak my piece before you go saying something you might regret." He rubbed the stubble on his chin, fingered the bandage on his head.

"Now, Judge Quinliven, he's a real hard rock. Not one to miss much. Wants to do things real thorough. Less chance of having one of his decisions overturned or tossed out, you see. So I'd imagine that if he heard Jace Martin point a finger at some other man, and heard a couple of deputies say that the real culprit was dead, he'd want to make sure. He'd send a bunch of miners and lawmen with picks and shovels and a coffin to bring back the dead robber's remains. And if that body wasn't found . . . well, that would mean more witnesses had to be called, more affidavits signed, things like that. Right cumbersome. Time consuming. A pain in the arse for a lawman."

He paused and leaned. He spit. He wiped his mouth.

"But the judge, he's practical, too. I mean, after all, it's Jace Martin who would be on trial, and not some dead man, or a man who ain't dead. So if that fellow that had been accused was nowhere to be found in the territory, and seeing that the man doing the accusing was bound to be sentenced to hard time . . . well, I don't think anything would come of Jace Martin's accusations. Providing, of course, that this fellow who had been accused wasn't to show up in New Mexico Territory till the good judge had retired. But, well, he'd have to be out of the territory, out of my jurisdiction, you see."

MacKinnon turned and studied the lawman.

"Now." Bookbinder leaned forward in his chair. "I've been doing me some thinking. Ran it by Nikita, and he's in no hurry to get back to the reservation. We decided that maybe there's something to this game of baseball that you interrupted. So we're going to stay here, rest up, and take in that stump match. It got delayed, you know. Postponed, I guess is what they call it. On account of that interruption you and Jace Martin begun. And that little ballist and cowboy from Engle. What's the boy's name?"

"Gene," MacKinnon answered. "Gene Rhodes."

"Right. Anyway, this is Sunday. Can't play a ball game on the Sabbath, and they said they'd like to play it tomorrow, but I said they couldn't do that. It's likely to rain tomorrow. So everyone's agreed that the game will be resumed on Tuesday. Two o'clock in the afternoon. That'll get more folks time to come out and take in the show. And for the Río Hondo to get some more kegs of beer hauled over from Ruidoso."

Tobacco juice pinged against the side of the cuspidor.

"That means I wouldn't be leaving Roswell for Lincoln till Wednesday, first light. And I'd have to stop at Bonito City to see if Charley The Trey or any of the other witnesses to the robbery there could positively identify Jace Martin as one of the hooligans who perpetrated that crime. So I could get an indictment."

He nodded. "Now that's about a two, three days' ride. Preliminary hearing wouldn't be able to convene till . . . I'd reckon, a week from tomorrow. Maybe even later, depending on how busy the judge, and I, happen to be."

He pushed himself to his feet, bent to move the cuspidor back where he had found it, and turned to find his hat. With his back to MacKinnon, he said: "You and Miss Callahan did not make good time in those two weeks you were leading her to Roswell. I trust you could move things along if you had half a mind to help her get to Texas."

"Texas?" MacKinnon's brow knotted.

"Yeah." Bookbinder nodded out the window. "That young woman, her sister, and baby brother are heading out today."

"What?" MacKinnon grimaced.

"Easy, bub. Don't bust your ribs any more

than you've already done." Bookbinder wiped his mouth and said: "I don't know where Miss Callahan got the notion to head off to Texas, but you know women. Or at least one woman. Yes, sir, MacKinnon, she and her siblings are bound for Texas. Today. Folks tried to talk them out of it, but she's as mule-headed as you are. Three or four eligible bachelors asked to assist her, but she said no. Doesn't have one notion where she's bound for, other than she's heading to Texas. And from there? Who knows? Hard to figure a girl like that, but I figure . . . mind you, this is just my opinion . . . that if you and that sorrel of yours was to volunteer, she'd say yes. In a heartbeat."

Gently, Bookbinder set his hat on his head, carefully pulling it just to the top of the white bandage.

"Ninety miles east is Texas," Bookbinder said. "My appointment as a deputy marshal is for this territory only. Least, that's the way I see it. You could be there by the time Jace Martin's spitting out his flapdoodle to Judge Quinliven. And if you rode south, just followed the Pecos, it's a tad longer, but the water's good, and I don't think anybody would suspect to look for some fellow accused of a crime taking that long way. Wouldn't make a lick of sense. Wouldn't make sense for that gent to keep moseying with that young lady and her two siblings all the way to Fort Davis. Davis Mountains, if you ask me, that's the prettiest piece of Texas there is. Only part of Texas worth living in. And there's a rancher I know, Clay Mundy, runs the Rafter Nine. He's always looking for a good cowpuncher. They've got an Army post there, so there's plenty of jobs to be found for a young lady with plenty of sand. And a school. For a red-headed sister and a brother who's just cute as a button. And this Mundy I was telling you about, well, he's even been known to help out a cowboy, stake him to some cattle, let him file a homestead claim. Understand, he does this so he has more land for his cattle. Deeded land. But it's something to think about. Especially if that cowboy was wanting to get married."

MacKinnon grimaced but managed to sit up in his bed. "Marry?" he said, and wrapped his arm around his ribs.

"I'm just thinking out loud, son."

"Marshal, I'm practically old enough to be her pa."

"But you ain't her pa, MacKinnon. And my pa was twenty-nine years older than my ma. They loved one another, though. That's what mattered."

"Love?" MacKinnon shook his head. "I'm a thirty-a-month-and-found saddle tramp."

"You're a good man," Bookbinder said, and laughed. "Good Sam MacKinnon." His head nodded. "You said that in your sleep. I liked it."

He shifted to spit. "Son, it might not take . . . you and her together. Hell, boy, y'all haven't known each other but a few days. Sometimes that's all it takes. Sometimes, it don't work out. But some things are worth trying. Some things, you just have to give a whirl."

"Bookbinder, if you know all the mistakes I've made . . ."

"I've made more than you, Good Sam MacKinnon. 'Course, I'm older than you. We all make fool choices. We all do foolish things. Some mistakes we forget. Most we learn from. But then there's some mistakes . . . like trying to rob a saloon, or something like that, something criminal . . . that most people have to pay for. There's no getting over that kind of mistake. Then it's too late. And even worse, there's the mistake countless folks make. They let somebody get away from them. And then it's too late. For both of them."

He nodded, turned, and pulled open the door. "That's a mistake I wouldn't want to live with for the rest of my life."

The door closed behind him.

CHAPTER TWENTY-NINE

The horses stood in front of the hitching rail at Peñalos's Feed and Grain. Nelson Bookbinder sat on the front bench, whittling. Beside him sat Nikita, hat brim pulled down over his eyes.

The knife stopped moving, and Bookbinder leaned forward. "Well," he said, "that old boy's got sense after all."

Nikita pushed up his hat, and stared across the street.

They watched as the red-headed sister took the sorrel and tied it behind the wagon, on the left side. On the right, they had already tied up that blind mule. Then all three—Florrie, Gary, and Katie—helped MacKinnon as he used a cane to ease his way out of The Holland House, onto the street, and into the new wagon. He sat on the tailgate, legs and boots dangling, and the boy jumped up beside him. The kid must have said something, because they could hear Sam MacKinnon laugh as he reached out to massage his ribs, and then brought his hand up to tousle the kid's hair.

Giggling, the boy handed MacKinnon a Beadle & Adams novel. MacKinnon looked, shook his head, opened the book, and started reading. It was one of those crazy adventures about a marshal named Bookbinder and an Apache scout with a Russian name. Bookbinder had bought it at the mercantile, then gave it to Gary as a present.

The two girls came to the front of the wagon, and climbed into the driver's box. Two big Percherons, wearing the brand of John Wesley Pringle's outfit, pulled the new wagon onto the dusty main street of Roswell. A few people stepped out of the buildings along both sides of the street, waving their hats or hands, some of them calling out fond farewells.

"The girl's driving?" Nikita said.

"That's a woman, Nikita. Not a girl. And women can drive a team," Bookbinder told him. He started to whittle again, but had to look up, and watch the *family* . . . yeah, that was the word he wanted . . . leave Roswell.

They rode east, but when they reached the banner at the end of town that proclaimed the **ENGLE VERSUS ROSWELL—ANNUAL STUMP MATCH**, the wagon turned south.

"Pecos River," Nikita said.

"I didn't hear you." Nelson Bookbinder stood, stretched, closed the blade of the pocket knife, and slipped it into his vest pocket.

"Let's go, Nikita."

"Go?" The Apache stared in disbelief. "Go where?"

"Home." Bookbinder went to his horse,

gathered the reins, found the stirrup, and stepped into the saddle.

"What about him?" The Apache pointed at the tails of the blind mule and the sorrel mare before both disappeared behind Florencio's Café. "What about Martin?"

After settling into the saddle, Nelson Bookbinder found his newly purchased plug of chewing tobacco. He peeled back the paper, and bit off a substantial chaw. "I'll send a deputy to fetch Jace Martin to Lincoln," Bookbinder said. "In a week or two."

The lawman turned his horse, kicked it gently, and rode down the dusty street toward the sinking sun.

Sighing, Nikita ducked underneath the hitching rail, grabbed his hackamore, and pulled the horse into the street. He looked over his shoulder. People disappeared inside their businesses, while a few kids gathered up the bunting that had blown down, and stuffed that into wheat sacks. The banners that stretched across the street popped in the wind.

Bringing both hands to his mouth as a cup, Nikita called out to the lawman: "Bookbinder! Aren't we going to stay for that baseball game?"

Author's Note

While I was writing drafts of the last few chapters of this novel, the editor of *Pasatiempo*, the Friday arts supplement of the *New Mexican*, Santa Fe's daily newspaper, asked if I would contribute to a special project. *Pasatiempo* was running a feature that would consist of short vignettes about New Mexico authors written by New Mexico authors. In short, the editor wanted a New Mexico writer to contribute an essay of between one hundred and fifty and three hundred words about another New Mexico writer's work and why that writer and work inspired and influenced that particular New Mexico writer.

A lot of writers were being sought out for the project, but let's face it—a lot of New Mexico writers are inspired and influenced by many of the same writers and works: Edward Abbey (*The Brave Cowboy*) . . . Rudolph Anaya (*Bless Me, Ultima*) . . . Richard Bradford (*Red Sky at Morning*) . . . Max Evans (*The Hi Lo Country*) . . . T.T. Flynn (*The Man from Laramie*) . . . Erna Fergusson (*Dancing Gods*) . . . Fred Grove (*The Great Horse Race*) . . . Tony Hillerman (any of his Joe Leaphorn/Jim Chee Navajo mysteries—*Dance Hall of the Dead* remains my favorite) . . . Paul Horgan (*A Distant Trumpet*) . . . Paul

Andrew Hutton (*The Apache Wars: The Hunt for Geronimo, the Apache Kid and the Captive Boy Who Started the Longest War in American History*) . . . Oliver La Farge (*Laughing Boy*) . . . Cormac McCarthy (*The Road*) . . . N. Scott Momaday (*House Made of Dawn*) . . . John Nichols (*The Milagro Beanfield War*) . . . Ernie Pyle (*Brave Men*) . . . Conrad Richter (*The Sea of Grass*) . . . Luke Short (*Blood on the Moon*) . . . Marc Simmons (*Kit Carson and His Three Wives: A Family History*) . . . Frank Waters (*The Man Who Killed the Deer*) . . . Norman Zollinger (*Meridian*) . . . and many others, including Willa Cather. She's mostly regarded as a Nebraska author, but one would have to include her *Death Comes for the Archbishop* when considering great New Mexico–set works.

Who do you pick?

The editor had a recommendation, asking if I might be willing to tackle Eugene Manlove Rhodes.

What a break! Actually, I replied, I was already considering him as my choice. It was a fortuitous suggestion. *MacKinnon* was inspired by Eugene Manlove Rhodes, or, more specifically, the novella the section editor wanted me to write about.

Many years ago, my literary agent, the late Jon Tuska, mailed me a videocassette of *Four Faces West*, a 1948 Western starring Joel McCrea.

Tuska knew of my interest in film, and whenever he had duplicates or was upgrading from VHS to DVD, he would send me what he no longer needed. One night, I plugged in the tape.

Four Faces West was based upon a novella by Rhodes, *Pasó Por Aqui*, originally serialized in 1926 in the *Saturday Evening Post*.

I already knew of Rhodes. After all, C.L. Sonnichsen, the great historian of the Southwest, had dedicated an entire chapter to Rhodes in his 1960 book *Tularosa: Last of the Frontier West* (I suppose you could include Doc Sonnichsen in your list of New Mexico literary greats. Although he was born in Minnesota and spent most of his writing life at the University of Texas at El Paso and at the *Arizona Journal of History* in Tucson, he did write a lot about New Mexico.)

Sonnichsen labeled Rhodes "The Bard of the Tularosa," and Rhodes's life story intrigued me. Still, I never saw any need to read anything by Rhodes until I watched *Four Faces West*.

The movie starred Joel McCrea as a cowhand who robs a bank in New Mexico to help out his pa. Our outlaw/hero escapes, befriending an Eastern nurse (Frances Dee, McCrea's real-life wife) on her way west, and a Hispanic gambler (Joseph Calleia). The banker (John Parrish) wants his money back and the robber punished, so the new marshal, Pat Garrett (Charles Bickford), goes after the outlaw. So does a posse.

What struck me about director Alfred E. Green's movie was simple. This was a Western released in 1948 in which Mexicans are depicted with decency and integrity. This also was a Western released in 1948—a year that saw rather hard-edged Western films such as *The Treasure of the Sierra Madre*, *Red River*, *Yellow Sky*, *Coroner Creek*, *Blood on the Moon*, and *Station West*, the latter with one of the most brutal fistfights you'll see in any Western—in which nobody dies. Not only that, not one shot is fired and not one punch is thrown in *Four Faces West*.

That intrigued me so much, I tracked down a copy of *Pasó Por Aqui*.

The title comes from a carving—loosely translated as "passed this way" or "passed by here"—at Inscription Rock at El Morro National Monument between Gallup and Grants in western New Mexico. As early as the 17th Century, travelers carved their names in the sandstone promontory. Zuni Indians called the place *A'ts'ina*, meaning "place of writings on the rock."

Four Faces West was mostly filmed in New Mexico, including around Gallup, El Morro, and White Sands National Monument in Alamogordo. Its national premiere was in Santa Fe.

The movie added the romance, stretched some things out, but, overall, remains fairly faithful to Rhodes's story. In both novella and film, the fleeing cowboy comes across a diphtheria-stricken Hispanic family, forcing our hero to make a choice. And just like in the movie, no shots are fired, no one dies, and no fisticuffs occur in the novella.

Eugene "Gene" Manlove Rhodes was born in Tecumseh, Nebraska, in 1869, but moved with his parents to southern New Mexico in 1881, where he worked as a stonemason and helped build roads. By the time he was thirteen, he was cowboying—and became a good one: "a reckless bronc buster," one person remembered, "a fanatic ball player and a fiend for poker and a fight."

He was also an avid reader—Lewis Carroll's *Alice in Wonderland* was a personal favorite. In an introduction to Rhodes's *The Proud Sheriff* (Houghton Mifflin, 1935), published the year after Rhodes's death, Henry Herbert Knibbs recounted an incident involving Rhodes, the cowboy/reader. Rhodes was riding a horse while reading a book, when the horse leaped, and both rider and mount fell down a ledge. When the colleagues finally reached them, they found both rider and horse banged up pretty good, but conscious.

"Hurt pretty bad?" one of the cowhands asked.

"No," Rhodes replied, "but, dammit, I lost my place in the story."

Grubstaked fifty dollars from his father in 1888, Rhodes entered the University of the Pacific, then located in San Jose, California, but two years of higher education was all he could afford, and he returned to New Mexico, "broke," Sonnichsen wrote, "and discouraged." In 1899, he married a widow, with whom he had corresponded and who admired his poetry. She tried to make it in and around Tularosa, but needed to return to New York to care for her mother. Three years later, in 1905, Rhodes joined his wife in New York. He remained exiled from his beloved New Mexico for some twenty years, but in New York, when he decided to write, he wrote about what he knew best.

Good Men and True, his first novel, was published in 1910. He wrote short stories, gaining notice for his works in the *Saturday Evening Post*, *The Land of Sunshine*, and *Out West*, the latter two edited by the renown Charles F. Lummis, and his novels.

In 1926, Rhodes and his wife returned to New Mexico, living in Santa Fe, Alamogordo, and at Albert Fall's "Rock House" at the Three Rivers Ranch.

Rhodes published roughly a dozen novels, including *West Is West* (1917), Stepsons of Light (1921), *Copper Streak Trail* (1924) and *The Trusty Knaves* (1933). His short stories and novellas totaled, depending on who's counting, around forty or sixty, and he penned many articles and book reviews. He also wrote a number of poems.

He might have become known as the "Cowboy Chronicler," but he wasn't giving readers shoot-em-ups. The *Los Angeles Times* called Rhodes "one of the few [Western writers] producing literature." Bernard De Voto said that Rhodes's stories reached "a level which it is intelligent to call art."

In 1930, suffering from a "bad heart" and after a bout with bronchitis, Rhodes left New Mexico for California—better health care—where he died in 1934. Per his request, he was buried in New Mexico. His grave is located just inside the gate of the White Sands Missile Range, between Socorro and Carrizozo, where the epitaph on his tombstone, fittingly, reads: *"Pasó por aquí."*

"He once said that his autobiography could be found in his books," Doc Sonnichsen wrote, "and this is simple truth. It is also true that much of the history of his time and place can be found there likewise."

I would have enjoyed meeting Gene Rhodes. When people asked where they could find him in Pacific Beach, California, Knibbs wrote, they would likely hear: "If he isn't at home, you'll find him at the baseball game."

Anyway, I drew from Eugene Manlove Rhodes when I started this novel. As a salute, I sprinkled a few names of characters from Rhodes's fiction for the population of Roswell.

I also remembered something Rhodes told

Knibbs: "They say I write pretty good stories. But nobody ever says what a good rider I was."

Nobody ever says what I good rider I am, either. Maybe for good reason.

The idea for the "broken ribs" plot element started percolating after a "horse wreck" near Ruidoso, New Mexico, in the summer of 2012.

Wally Roberts was living down in southern New Mexico at the time, where he catered rodeos and weddings and organized equine adventures through his company, Outlaws & Renegades, LLC. We had first met when *Western Horseman* magazine hired me as a photographer for an article to be written by Albuquerque journalist Ollie Reed, Jr. about a hard, and long, "Billy the Kid's Last Ride" trail ride that started in Lincoln and ended in Fort Sumner. A horse named Chuck, appropriately, chucked me off at a high lope during that assignment.

In 2012, Roberts invited me to come down to see what was involved in planning one of these "endurance" trail rides. It seemed like an intriguing idea for a magazine story, especially since the ride he was trying to make feasible would begin at the site of John Tunstall's dugout on the Felix Cañon Ranch in southern New Mexico. Tunstall, of course, became famous after he was murdered—a key incident in the Lincoln County War that propelled a young gunman to fame under his nickname, Billy the Kid.

Roberts put me on Honey, a five-year-old mare that his daughter rode and which, he told me, "has never gotten any rider in trouble."

For our "pre-ride," Roberts, Felix Cañon Ranch foreman Chris Mauldin, and I trailered the horses to Tunstall's murder site near Glencoe, unloaded them, and prepared to ride. As soon as I was in the saddle, Honey—who, remember, "has never gotten any rider in trouble"—started bucking.

Let the record show that I was not bucked off. Even Wally Roberts will testify to that. I stayed on for at least three jumps (all these years later, I'm thinking about making it four jumps). But when Honey decided to roll, I kicked out of the stirrups and dived in the opposite direction. My landing went, ribs-camera-rocks. Fearing that Honey might roll the other way, I got up, sort of, staggered a bit, and collapsed.

They caught Honey. I breathed. The filter on my camera lens was smashed, but the Canon still worked fine. Eventually, I sat up. Roberts checked my ribs. I didn't feel that bad, having not been rolled over by an angry mare.

Remembering the Code of the Cowboy, I climbed back into the saddle. We rode down to the marker at Tunstall's murder site, snapped some photos, and Roberts left me with Mauldin. Roberts would trailer his horse down the road and meet up with us as we came down the trail.

Only, there was no trail. Mauldin was trying

to find something paying customers could use. It did not take long until my right side began hurting. A lot. A short while later, I realized that I was in trouble. Just like Sam MacKinnon understands in this novel, I knew that if I climbed out of the saddle, I wouldn't be able to get back on. There would be a pretty good chance that I'd have to sit there till Roberts or medical personnel came to fetch me—and Ruidoso, the nearest city with a hospital, was about twenty-five miles west down the main road, U.S. Highway 70.

So when Mauldin dismounted to lead his horse down or up rock-strewn hillsides, or to duck underneath branches or limbs, I stayed in the saddle. I ducked—and, yeah, that hurt a lot—underneath branches. I twisted to keep from being knocked to the ground. Going uphill, I leaned forward; going downhill, I leaned back. Somehow, I didn't lose my seat.

Come to think on it all these years later, I am a pretty good rider. At the least, I am, as Roberts said later that day, one tough S.O.B.

Anyway, roughly ninety minutes later, Wally Roberts rode up to Mauldin and me, we found a bit of a trail, and rode back to the trailer, where I dismounted. Roberts again checked my ribs, gave me a bottle of water to drink, and he decided that maybe we should stop at this country store down the road and buy some Advil or Tylenol. When we reached camp, I could even wash those down with cold beer.

On that drive to the store, Roberts and Mauldin cracked a joke at my expense. I laughed, and spit up some of the water I was drinking. Roberts joked: "Johnny, you're not spitting up blood are you?"

When I checked—no blood—I noticed Roberts and Mauldin looking at one another.

That's when Roberts suggested that maybe, just to be safe, they ought to take me back to Ruidoso, get me in the E.R., make sure I was all right.

I said: "That's a pretty good idea."

The woman at the desk at the hospital asked for the time of the incident. I told her around 10:00 a.m. She gave me the incredulous look and said: "Why are you just getting here?" By then, it was around two in the afternoon.

I answered: "I had to finish the ride."

The first nurse to examine me saw the imprint left by the camera. "Here's the body. . . . Here's the lens."

X-rays and further examination brought in the doctor, who said: "Two fractured ribs. Stay off horses for a while."

When my wife learned what had happened, she suggested that I stay off horses permanently. I haven't. But, so far, I haven't been bucked off or injured in those past few years.

It turned out fine for everyone. Wally Roberts

got a new addition to one of his cookbooks, also at my expense: "Honey-braised ribs."

I used part of the busted-ribs adventure in my previous novel, *Taos Lightning*. But in *Taos Lightning* that fictional incident happens in Vermont.

Instead of New England, I wanted to set the entire story near Eugene Manlove Rhodes country (although I've placed this novel a little south and east of Engle, and a bit north and east of Alamogordo and Tularosa). Mostly, I wanted to stay faithful to Rhodes's vision of the West, and possibly reintroduce a new generation of readers to "The Bard of the Tularosa."

I've reread *Pasó Por Aqui* a number of times. Sure, the first two small chapters leave me scratching my head, and, especially to today's readers, his dialogue can feel dated. But the story is beautiful. The land is as much of a character as Ross McEwen, the cowboy turned outlaw, and Rhodes writes with a love of people and place— both of which he knew quite well.

I'm glad Tuska sent me that copy of *Four Faces West*. I'm happy that I had the good sense to buy a used copy of *Pasó Por Aqui* and become more acquainted with Eugene Manlove Rhodes.

As I wrote in *Pasatiempo*: "He passed this way. I'm glad he did."

Johnny D. Boggs
Santa Fe, New Mexico

ABOUT THE AUTHOR

Johnny D. Boggs has worked cattle, shot rapids in a canoe, hiked across mountains and deserts, traipsed around ghost towns, and spent hours poring over microfilm in library archives—all in the name of finding a good story. He's also one of two Western writers to have won seven Spur Awards from Western Writers of America (for his novels, *Camp Ford*, in 2006, *Doubtful Cañon*, in 2008, and *Hard Winter* in 2010, *Legacy of a Lawman*, *West Texas Kill*, both in 2012, *Return to Red River* in 2017, and his short story, "A Piano at Dead Man's Crossing," in 2002) as well as the Western Heritage Wrangler Award from the National Cowboy and Western Heritage Museum (for his novel, *Spark on the Prairie: The Trial of the Kiowa Chiefs*, in 2004). A native of South Carolina, Boggs spent almost fifteen years in Texas as a journalist at the Dallas *Times Herald* and Fort Worth *Star-Telegram* before moving to New Mexico in 1998 to concentrate full time on his novels. Author of dozens of published short stories, he has also written for more than fifty newspapers and magazines, and is a frequent contributor to *Boys' Life* and *True West*. His Western novels cover a wide range. *The Lonesome Chisholm Trail* (2000) is an authentic cattle-drive story, while *Lonely Trumpet* (2002) is an historical novel about the first black graduate of West Point. *The Despoilers* (2002) and *Ghost Legion* (2005) are set in the Carolina backcountry during the Revolutionary War. *The Big Fifty* (2003) chronicles the slaughter of buffalo on the southern plains in the 1870s, while *East of the Border* (2004) is a comedy about the theatrical offerings of Buffalo Bill Cody, Wild Bill Hickok, and Texas Jack Omohundro, and *Camp Ford* (2005) tells about a Civil War baseball game between Union prisoners of war and Confederate guards. "Boggs's narrative voice captures the old-fashioned style of the past," *Publishers Weekly* said, and *Booklist* called him "among the best Western writers at work today." Boggs lives with his wife Lisa and son Jack in Santa Fe. His website is www.johnnydboggs.com.

Center Point Large Print
600 Brooks Road / PO Box 1
Thorndike, ME 04986-0001 USA

(207) 568-3717

US & Canada:
1 800 929-9108
www.centerpointlargeprint.com